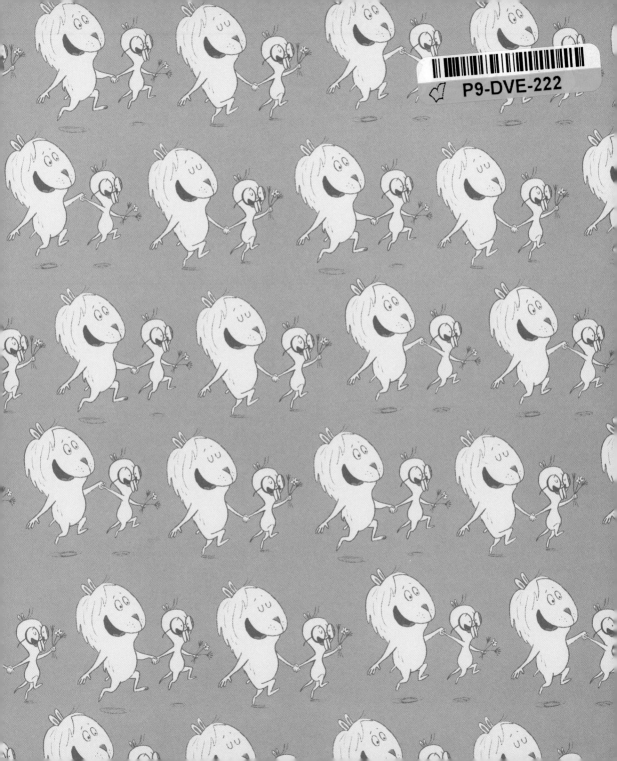

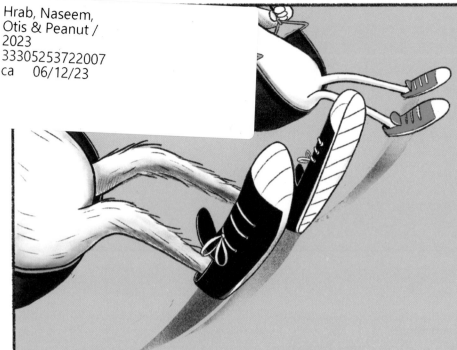

OTIS & PEANUT

WORDS BY
NASEEM HRAB

DRAWINGS BY
KELLY COLLIER

Owlkids Books

For Michelle, my forever first reader and friend —N.H.

To Mike, for always being there to help me solve problems and draw bicycles —K.C.

Text © 2023 Naseem Hrab | Illustrations © 2023 Kelly Collier

Owlkids Books acknowledges the financial support of the Canada Council for the Arts, the Ontario Arts Council, the Government of Canada through the Canada Book Fund (CBF) and the Government of Ontario through the Ontario Creates Book Initiative for our publishing activities.

Owlkids Books gratefully acknowledges that our office in Toronto is located on the traditional territory of many nations, including the Mississaugas of the Credit, the Chippewa, the Wendat, the Anishinaabeg, and the Haudenosaunee Peoples.

Published in Canada by Owlkids Books Inc., 1 Eglinton Avenue East, Toronto, ON M4P 3A1
Published in the US by Owlkids Books Inc., 1700 Fourth Street, Berkeley, CA 94710

Library of Congress Control Number: 2022939303

Library and Archives Canada Cataloguing in Publication

Title: Otis & Peanut / written by Naseem Hrab ; illustrated by Kelly Collier.
Other titles: Otis and Peanut
Names: Hrab, Naseem, author. | Collier, Kelly, artist.
Identifiers: Canadiana 20220261334 | ISBN 9781771474962 (hardcover)
Subjects: LCGFT: Graphic novels. | LCGFT: Comics (Graphic works)
Classification: LCC PN6733.H77 O85 2023 | DDC j741.5/971—dc23

Edited by Jennifer Stokes | Designed by Alisa Baldwin

A version of "The Haircut" appeared in the May 2021 issue of *Chirp* magazine as "Otis Needs a Haircut."

MIX
Paper from
responsible sources
FSC® C104723
www.fsc.org

Manufactured in Guangdong Province, Dongguan City, China, in September 2022, by Toppan Leefung Packaging & Printing (Dongguan) Co., Ltd.   Job #BAYDC118

A   B   C   D   E   F

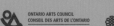
ONTARIO ARTS COUNCIL
CONSEIL DES ARTS DE L'ONTARIO
an Ontario government agency
un organisme du gouvernement de l'Ontario

Canada Council   Conseil des Arts
for the Arts   du Canada

Canada

Owl kids
Publisher of Chirp, Chickadee and OWL
www.owlkidsbooks.com

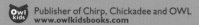
Owlkids Books is a division of

bayard canada

CONTENTS

THE HAIRCUT

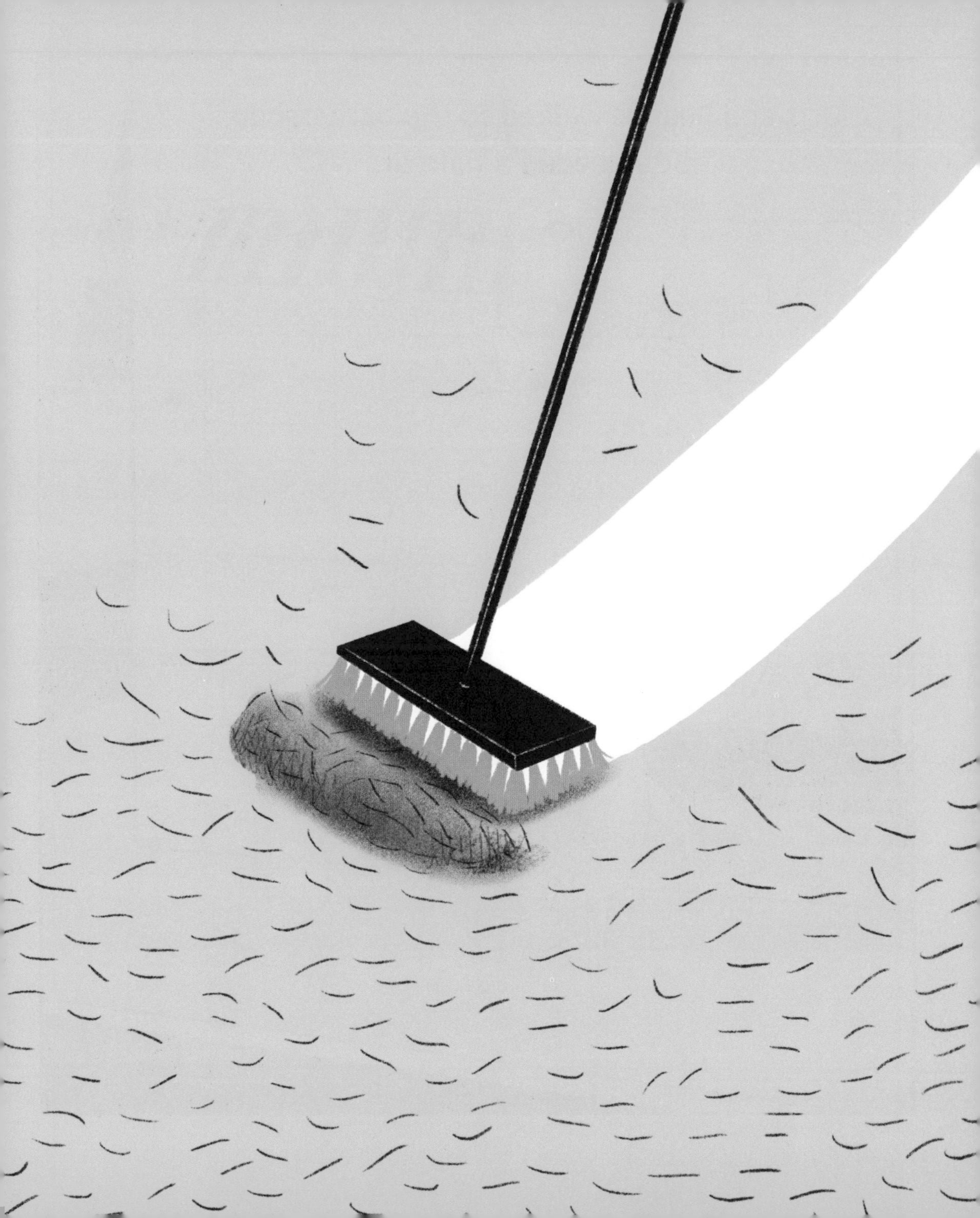

Otis and Peanut walked to the barbershop.
Otis needed a haircut.

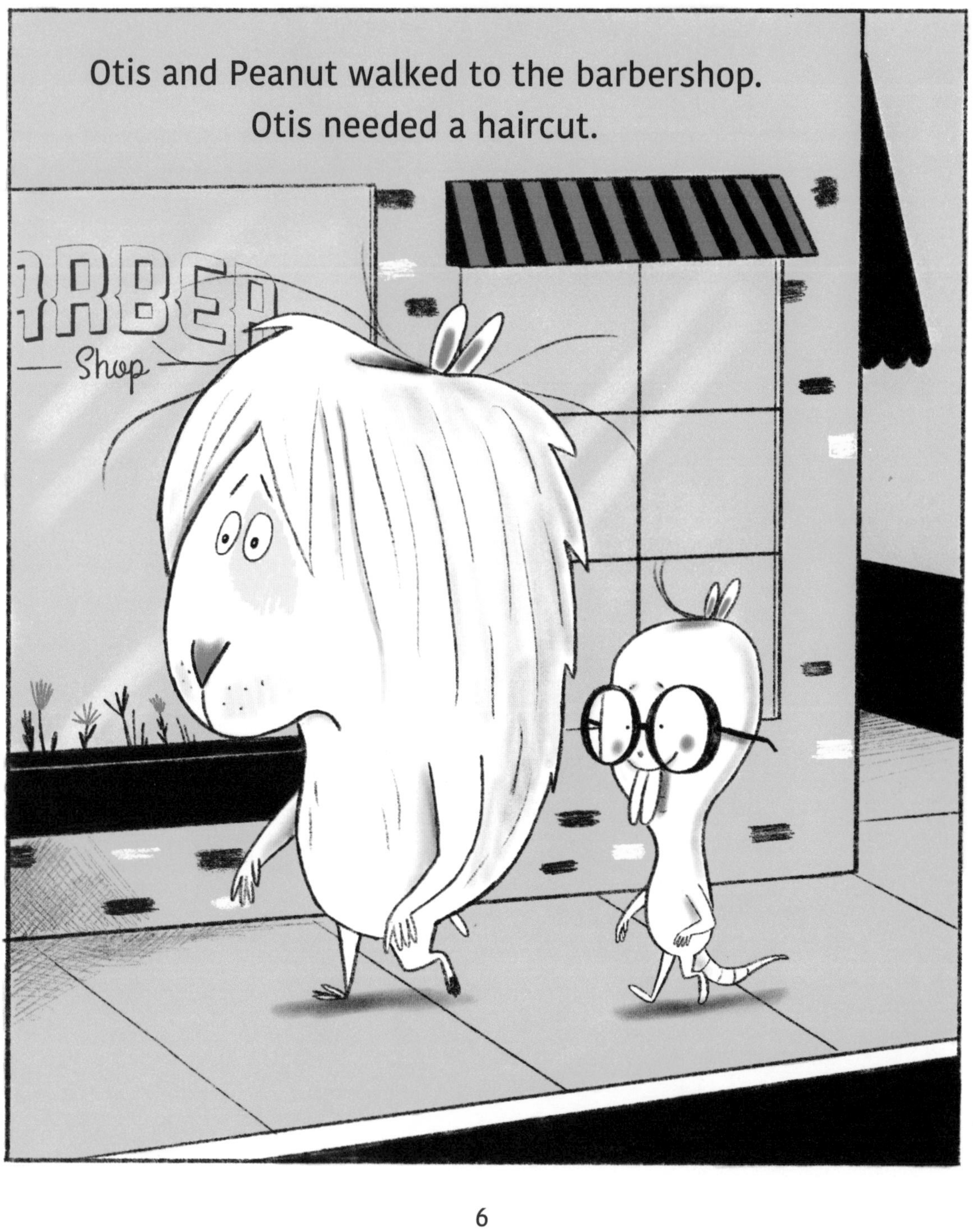
Shop

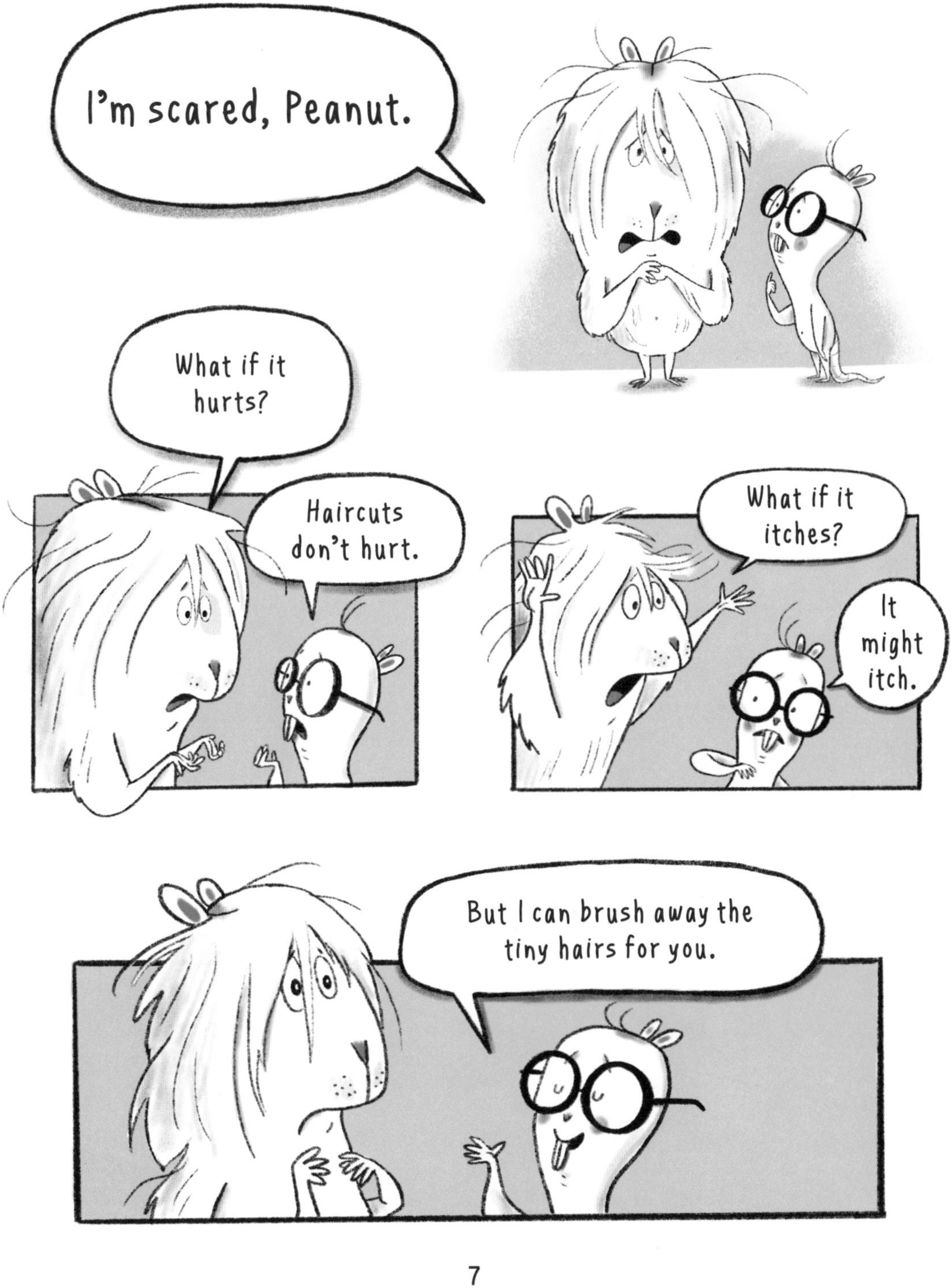
I'm scared, Peanut.
What if it hurts?
Haircuts don't hurt.
What if it itches?
It might itch.
But I can brush away the tiny hairs for you.

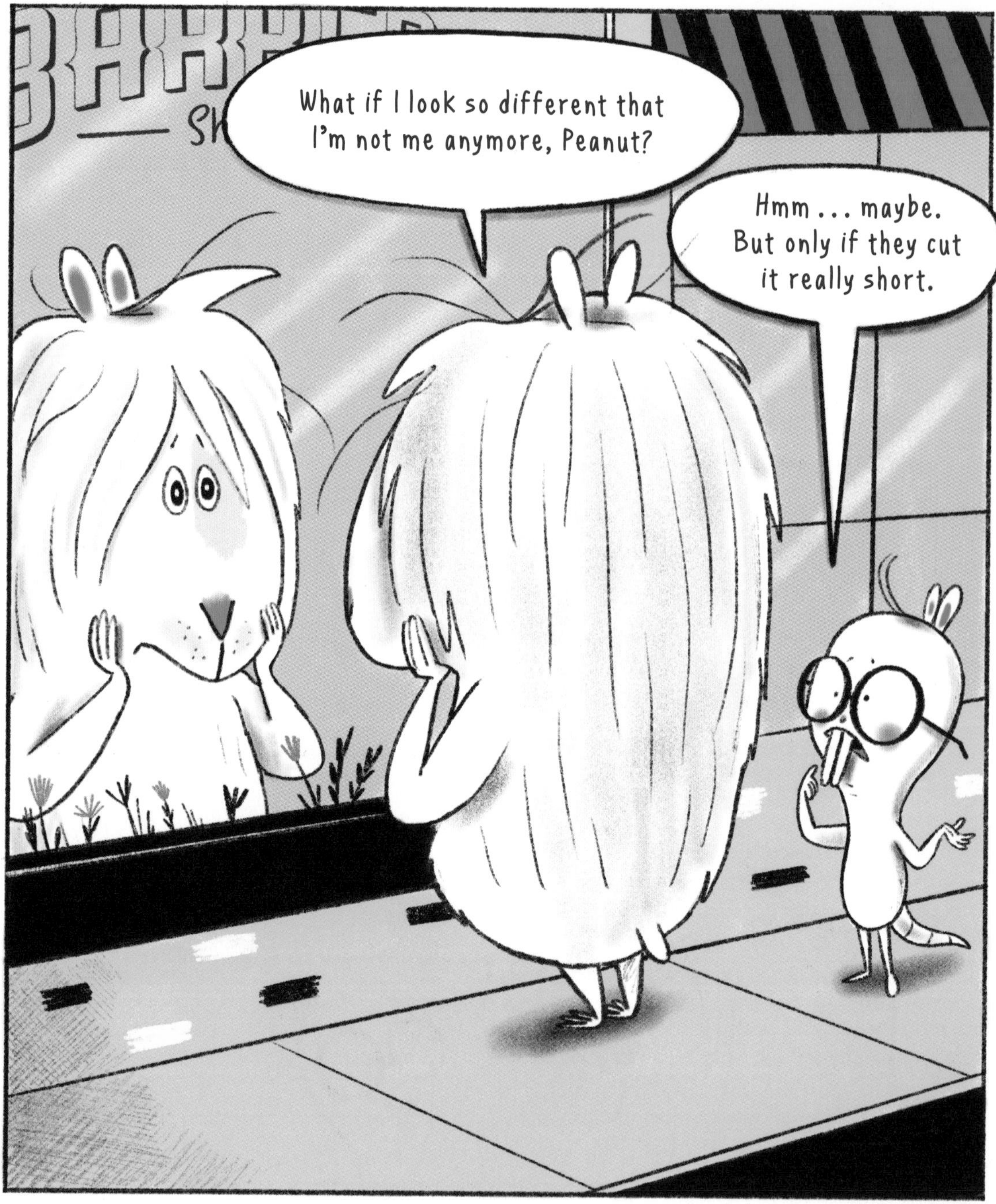
What if I look so different that I'm not me anymore, Peanut?
Hmm . . . maybe. But only if they cut it really short.

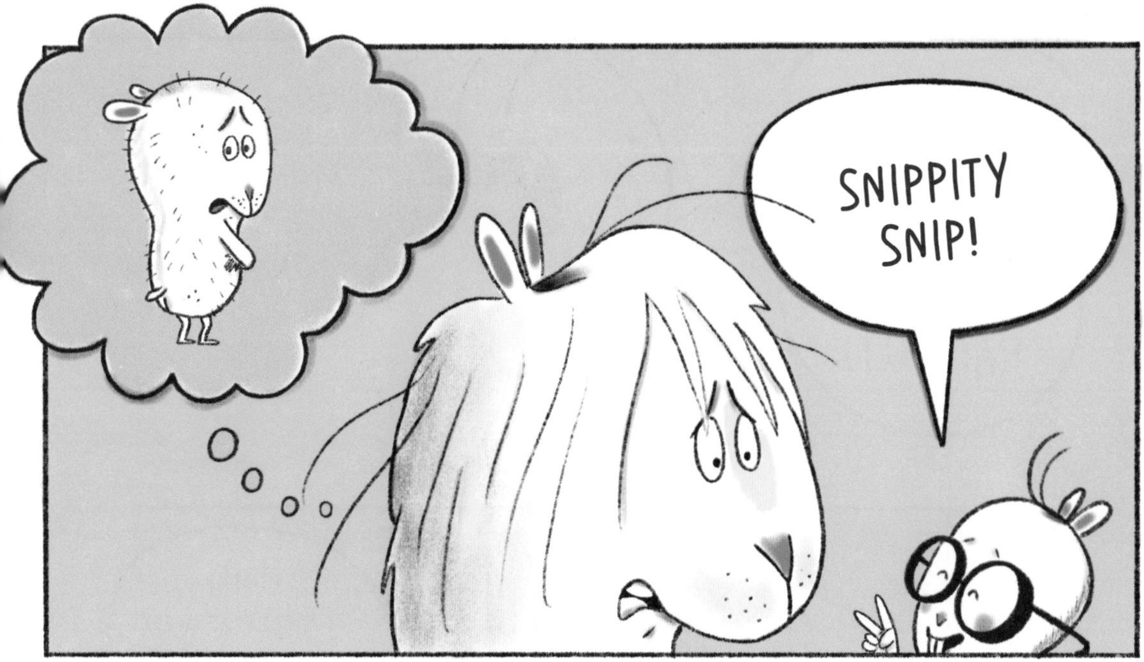
SNIPPITY SNIP!

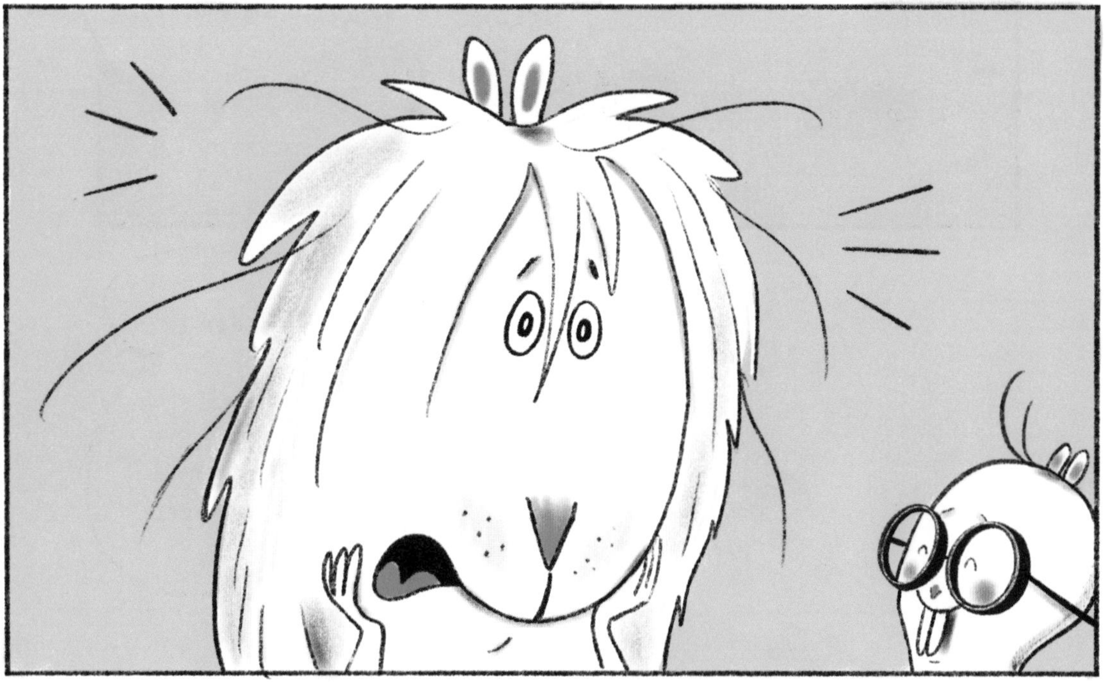

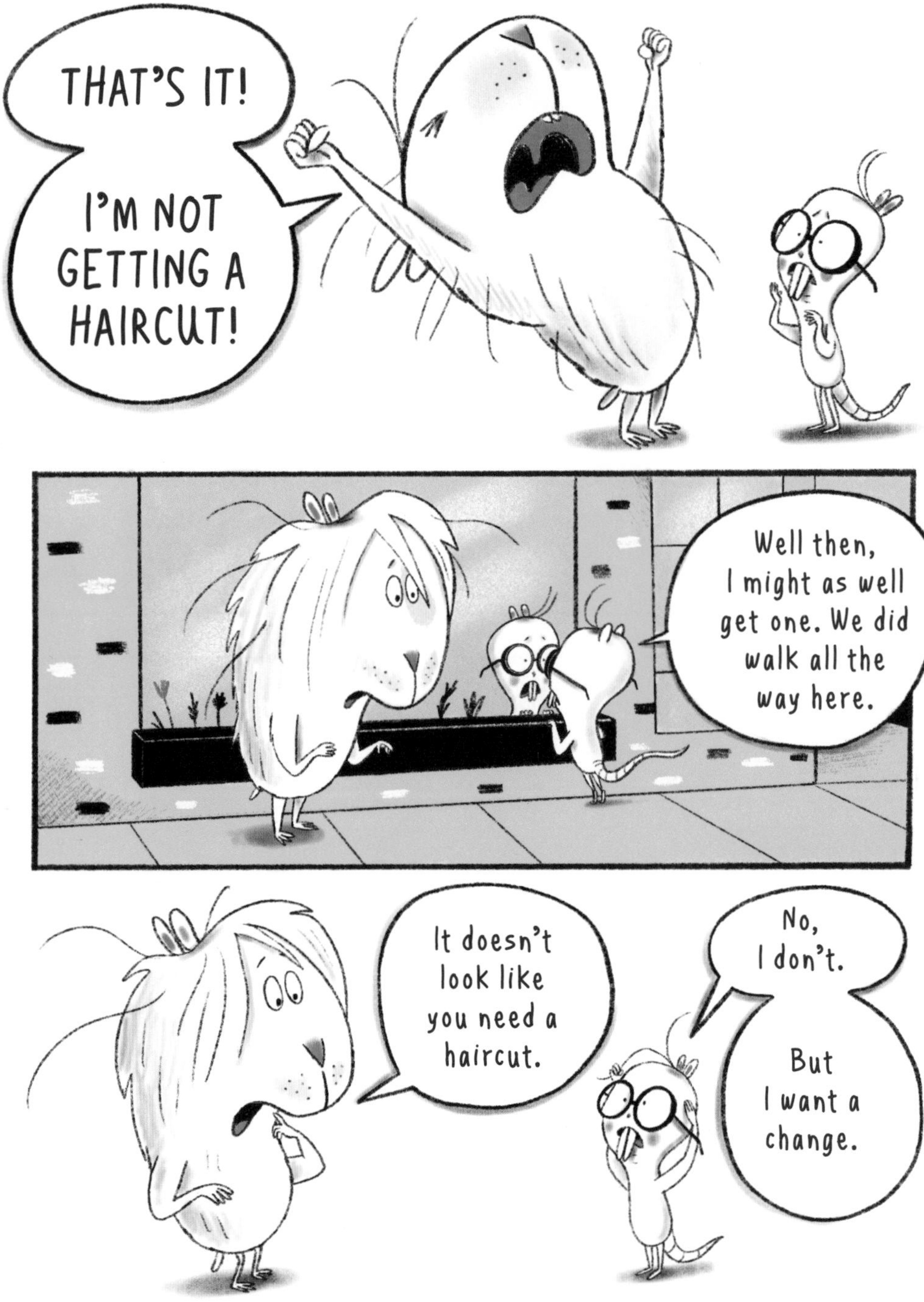
THAT'S IT!
I'M NOT GETTING A HAIRCUT!
Well then, I might as well get one. We did walk all the way here.
It doesn't look like you need a haircut.
No, I don't.
But I want a change.

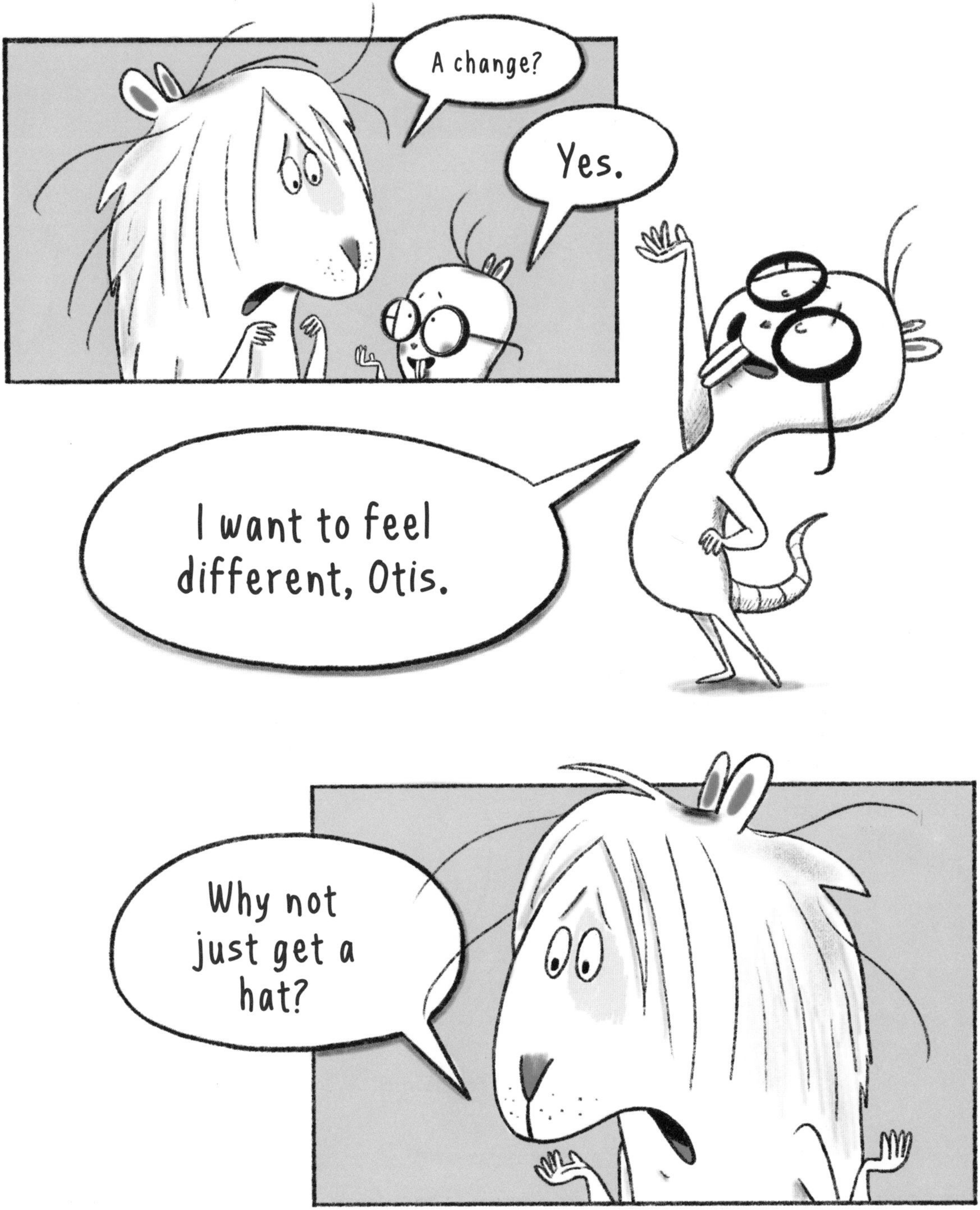
A change?
Yes.
I want to feel different, Otis.
Why not just get a hat?

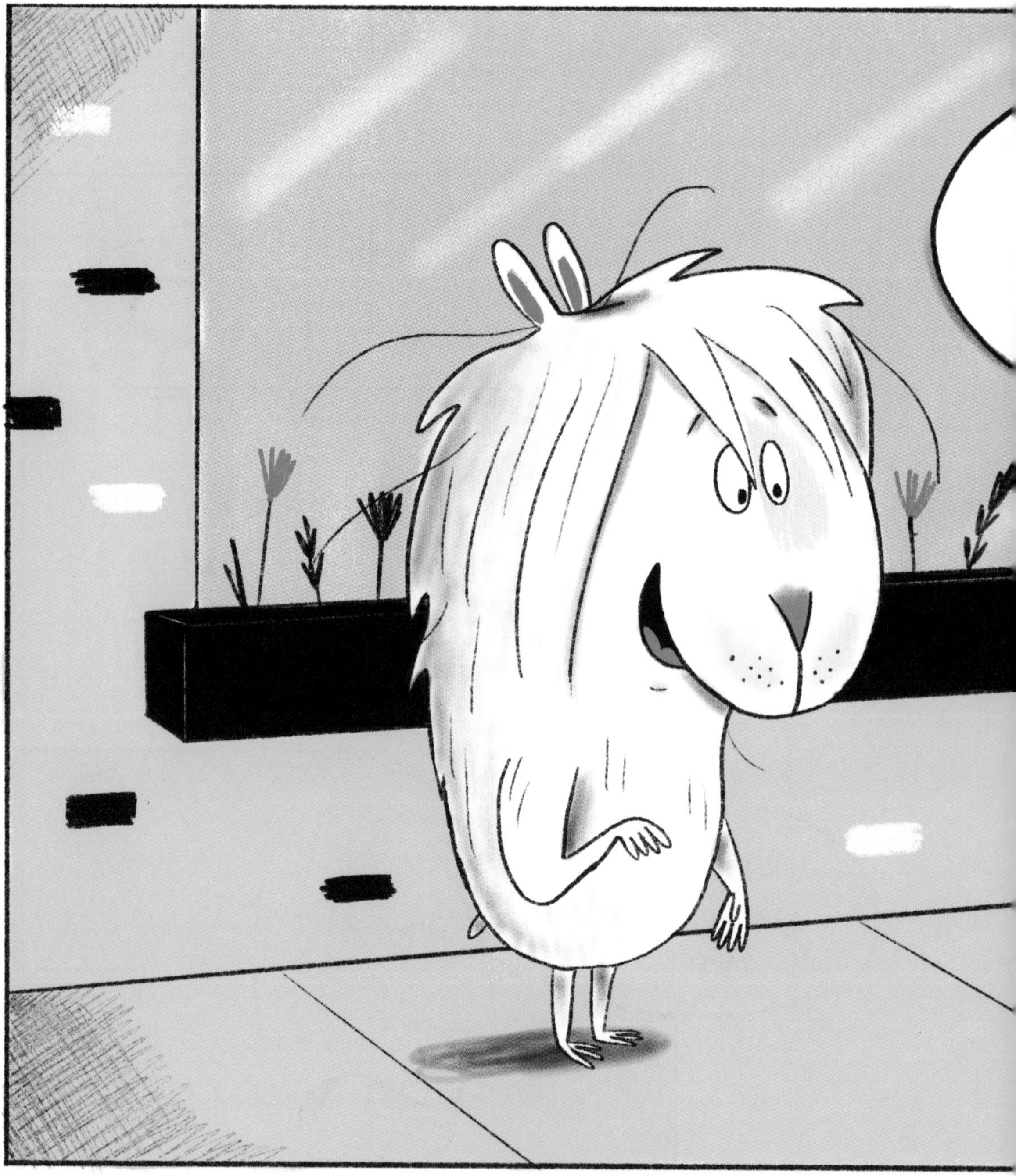

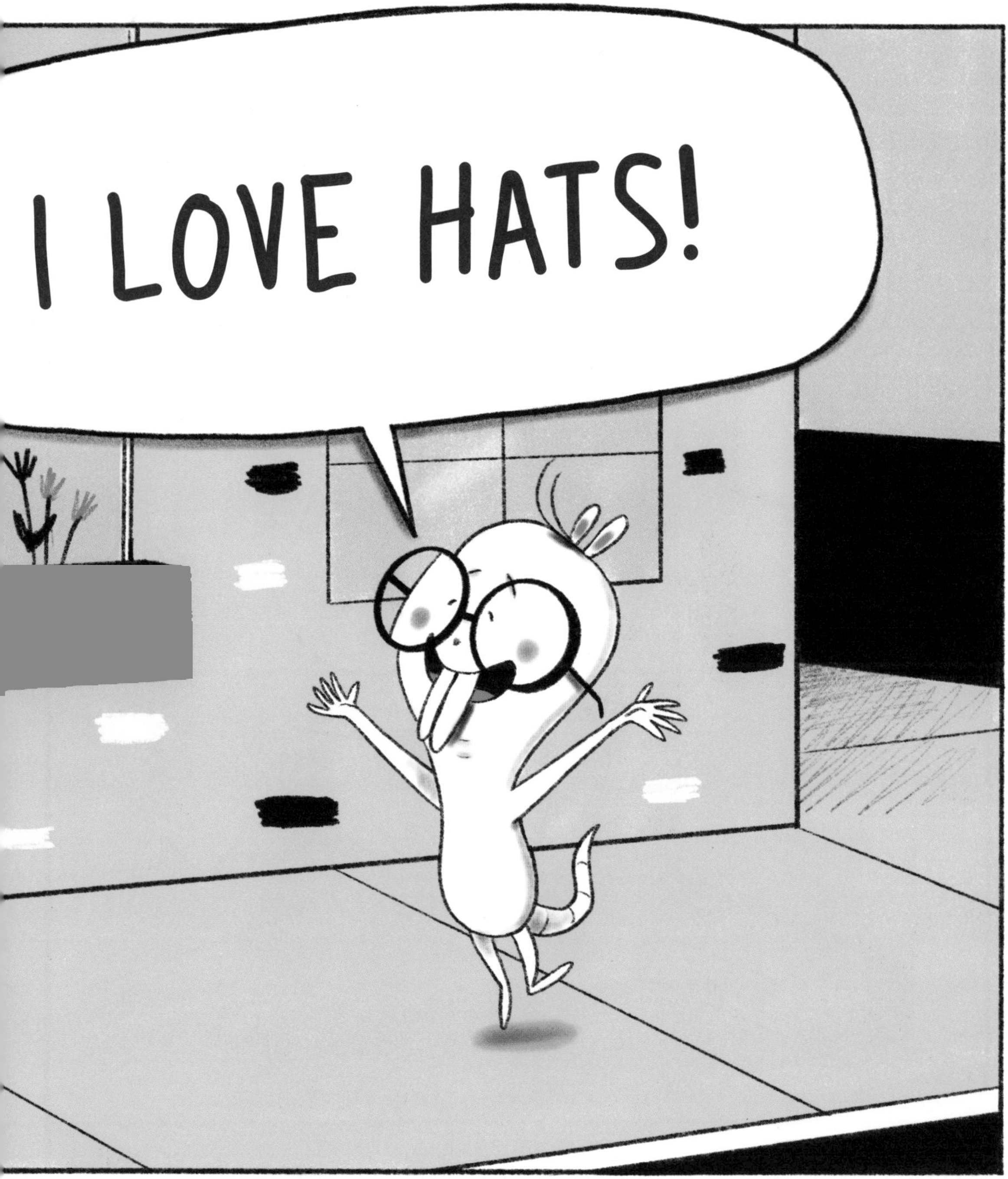
I LOVE HATS!

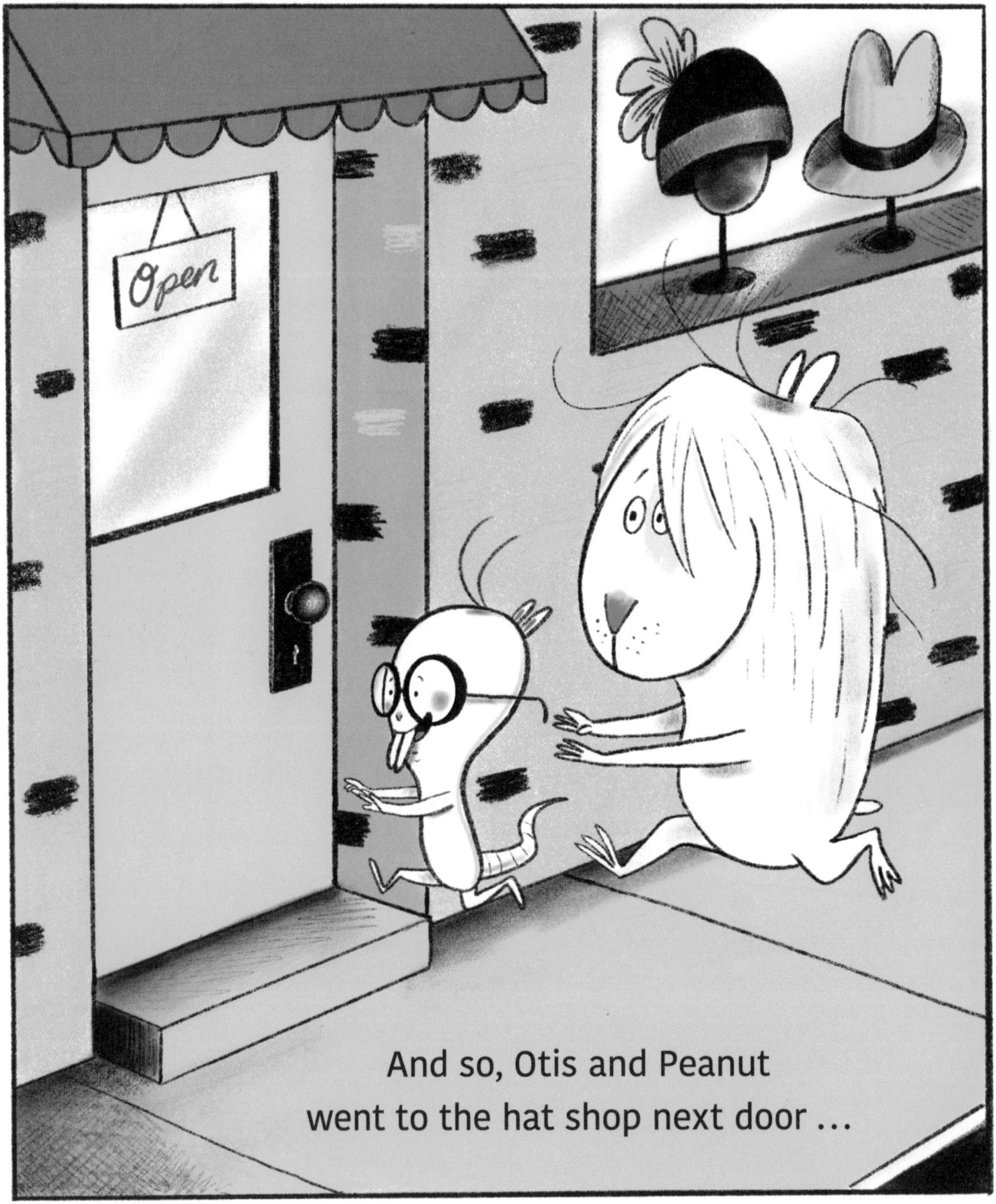
Open

And so, Otis and Peanut went to the hat shop next door …

and Peanut bought a blue felt hat.

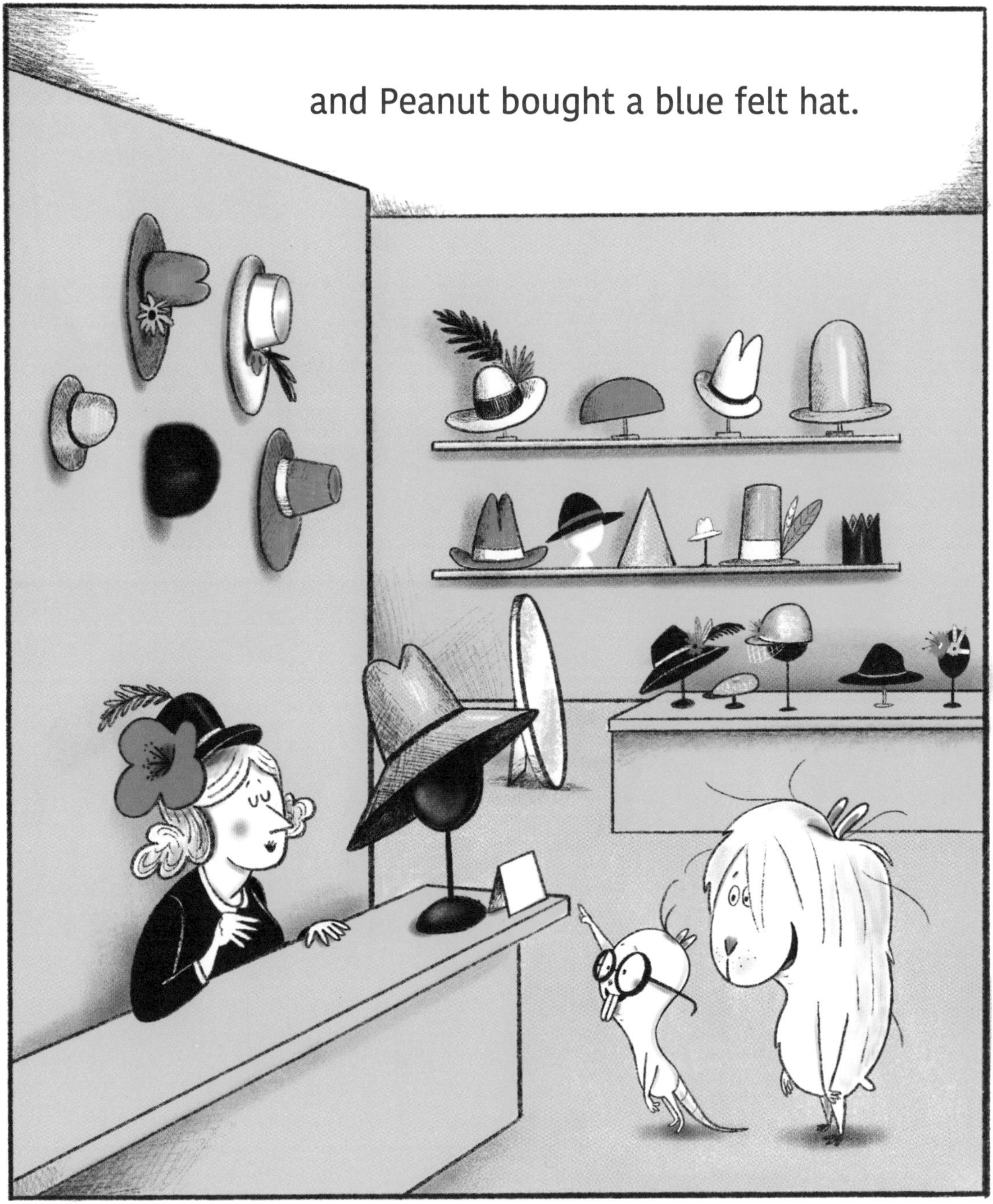

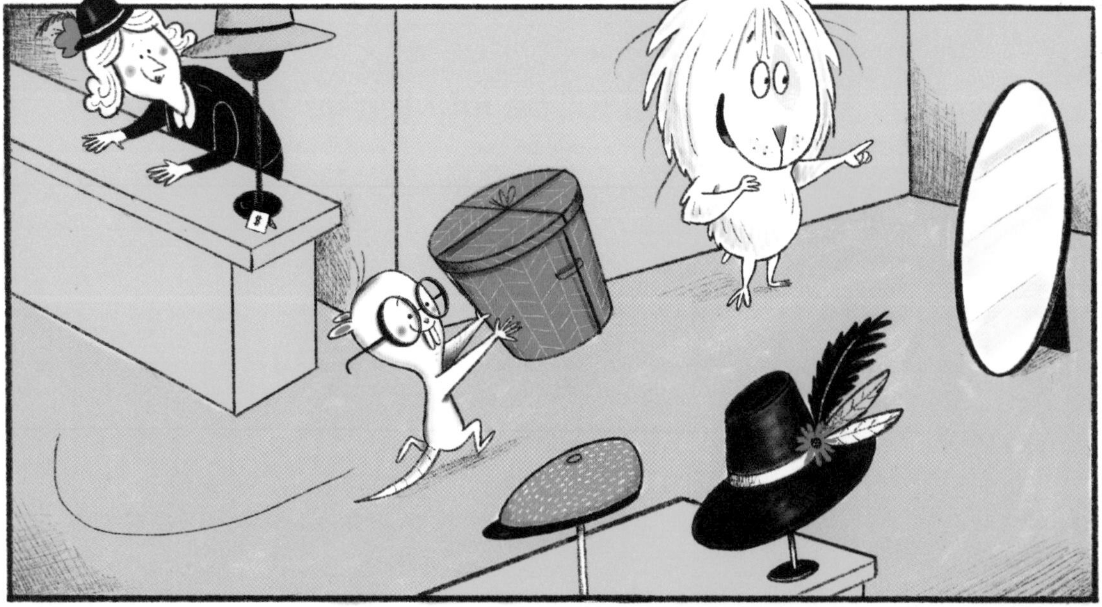

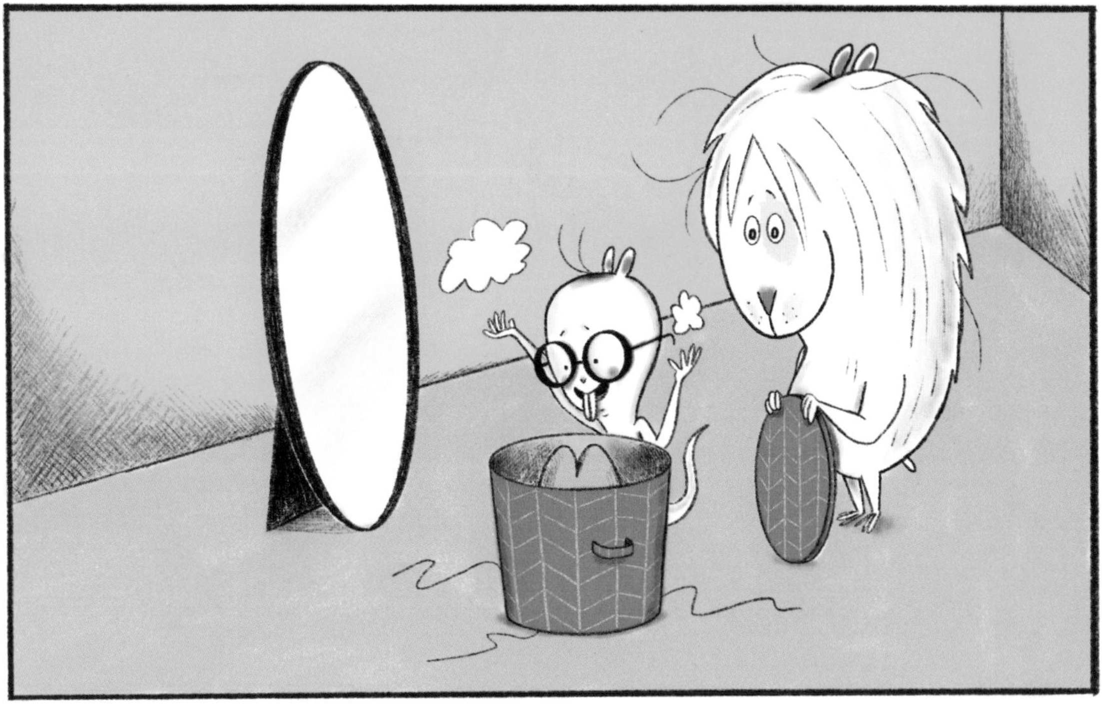

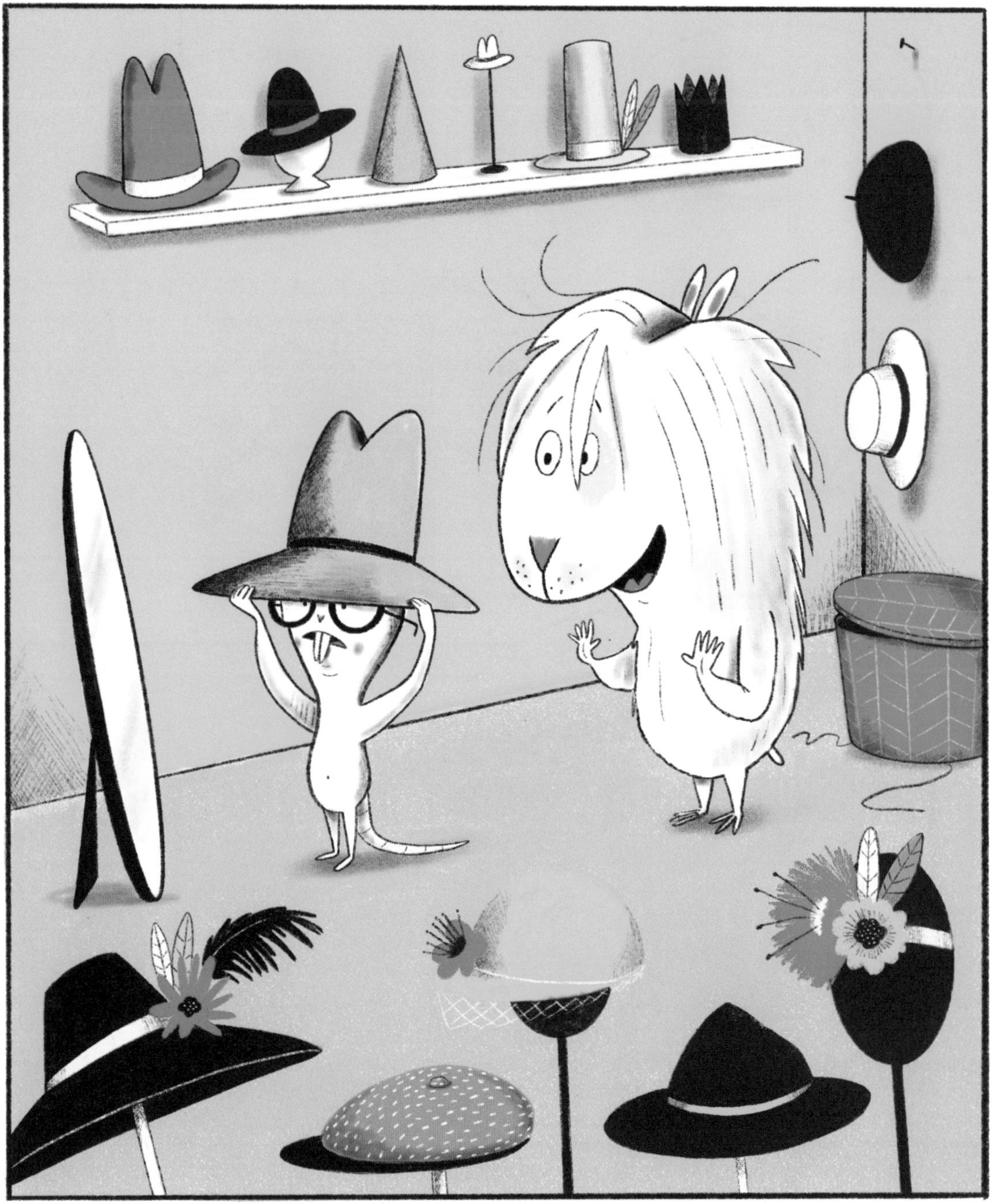

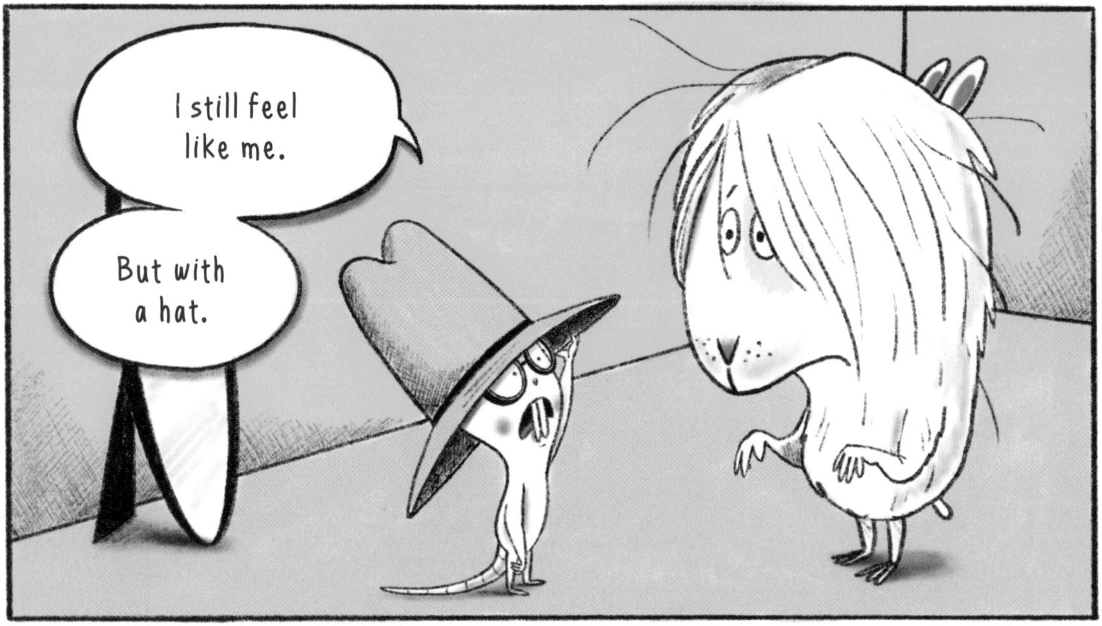
I still feel like me.
But with a hat.

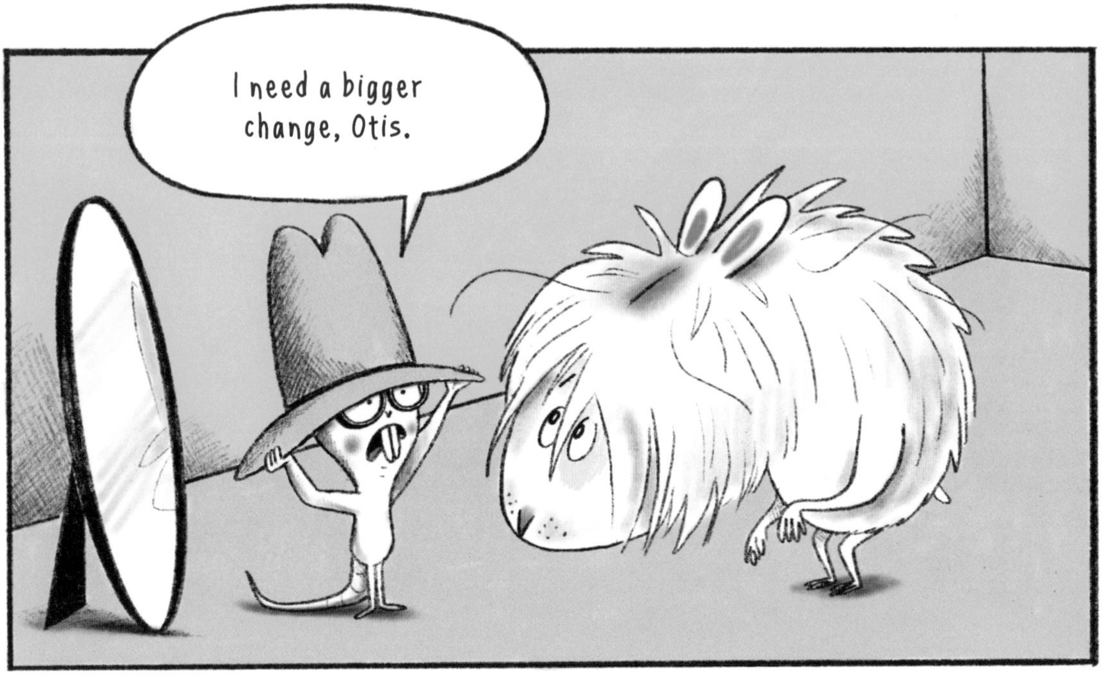
I need a bigger change, Otis.

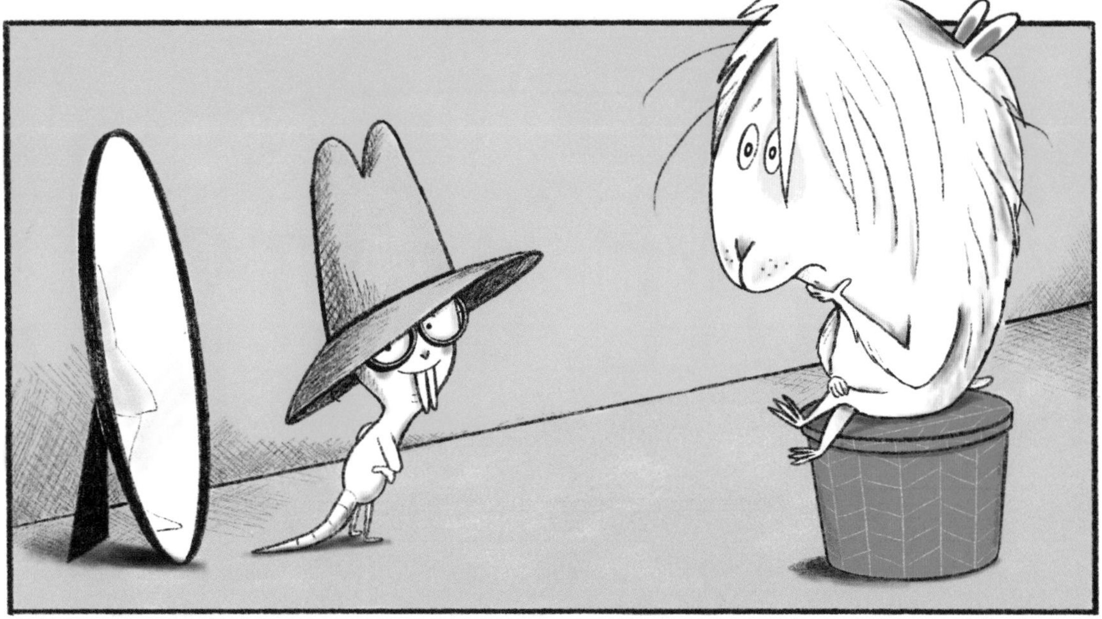

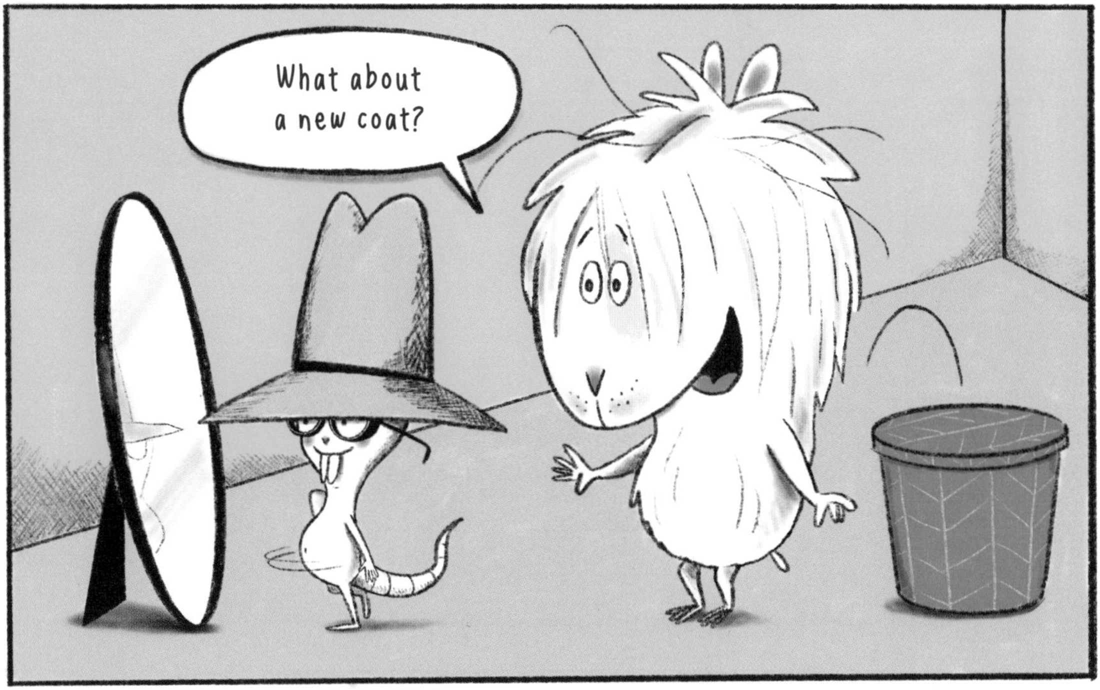
What about a new coat?

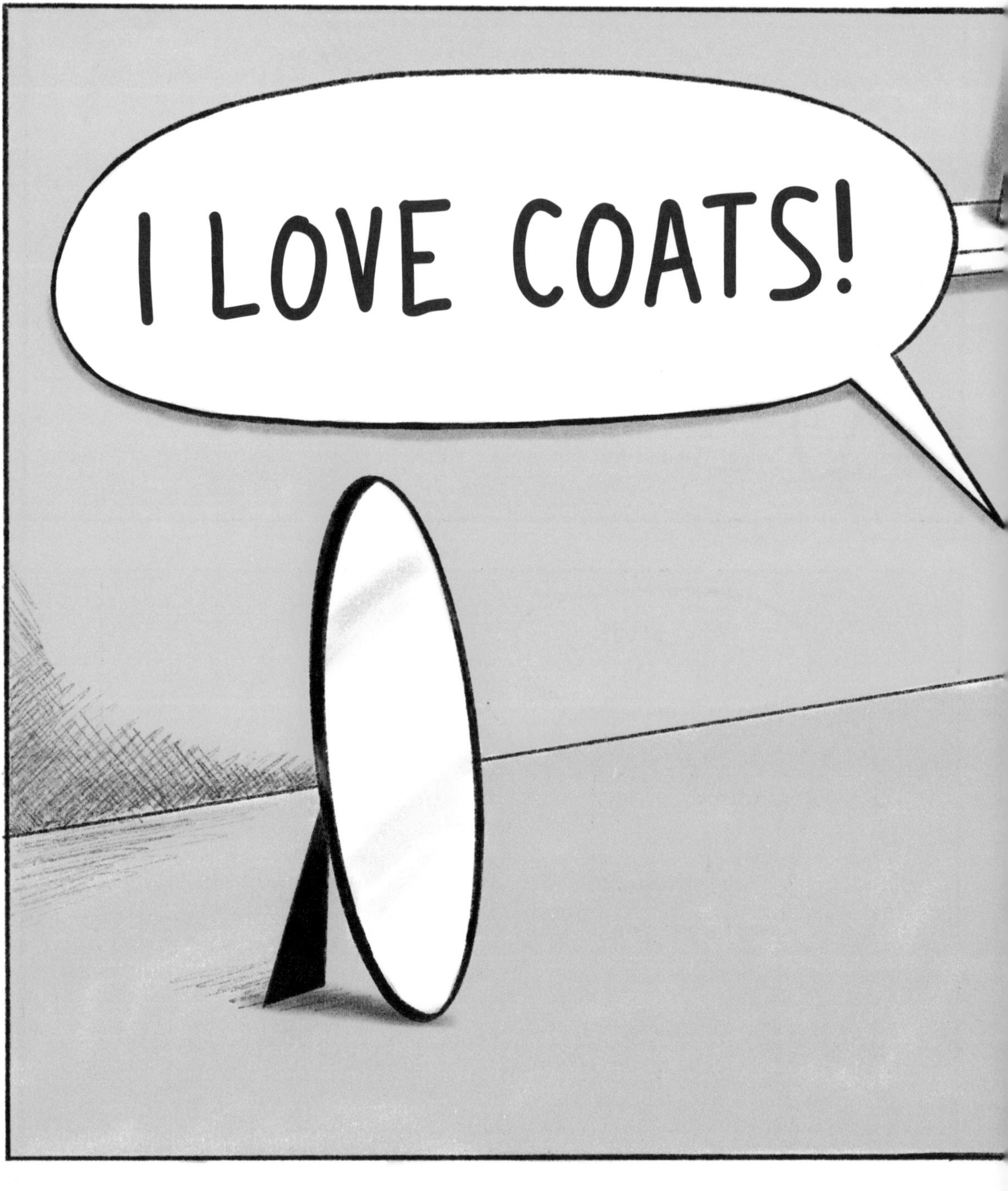
I LOVE COATS!

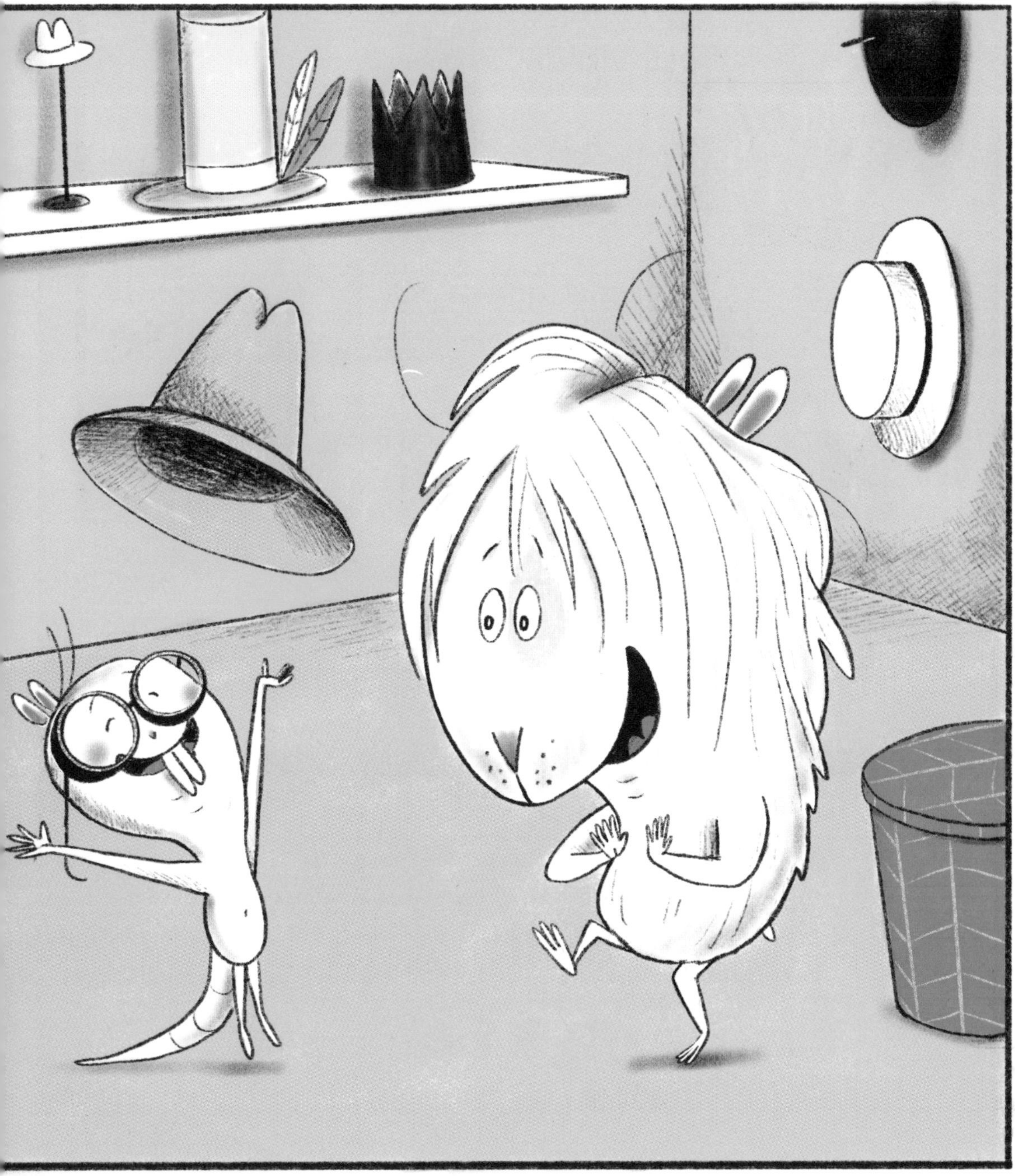

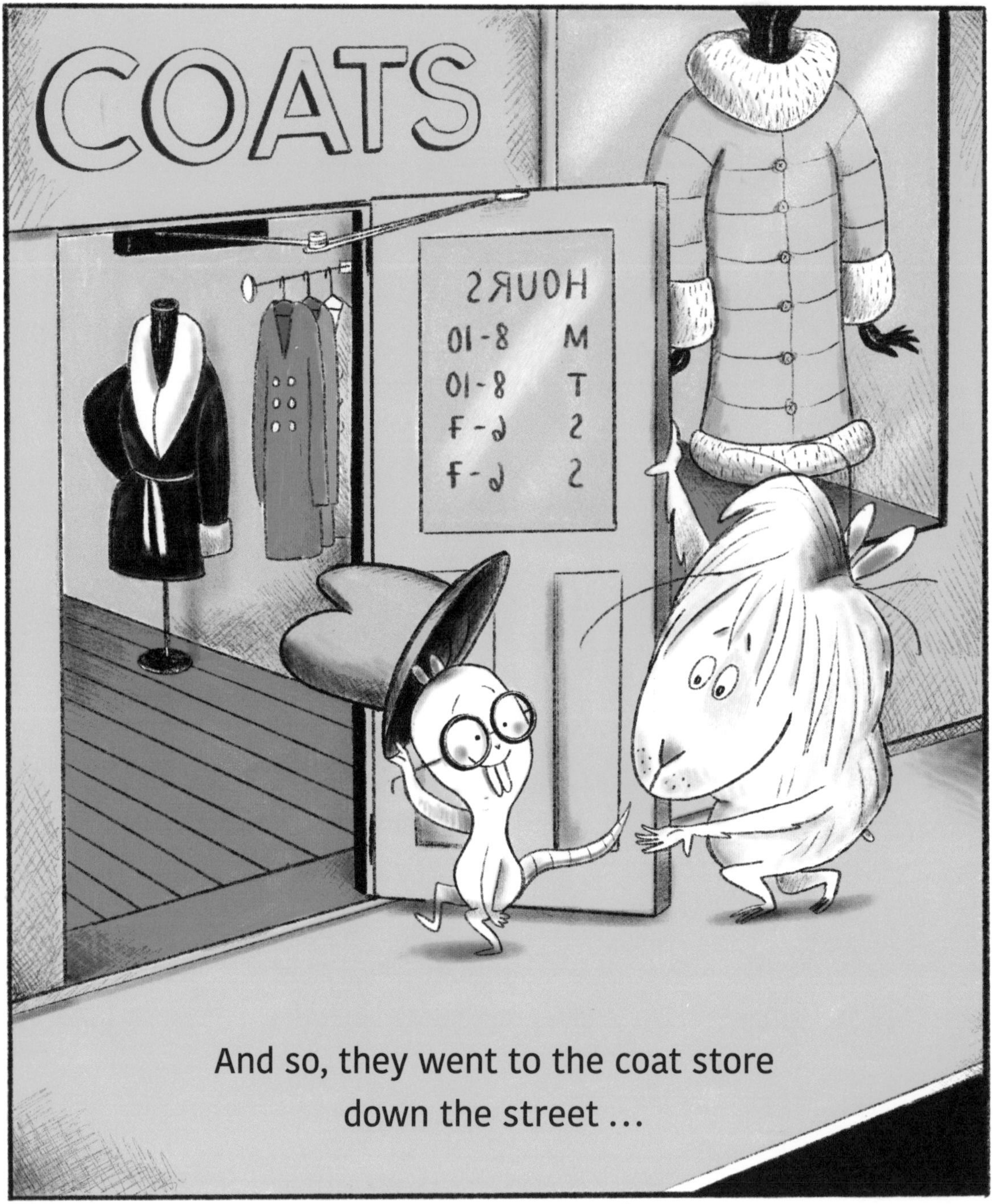
COATS
And so, they went to the coat store
down the street ...

and Peanut chose a yellow jacket with brown patches on the elbows.

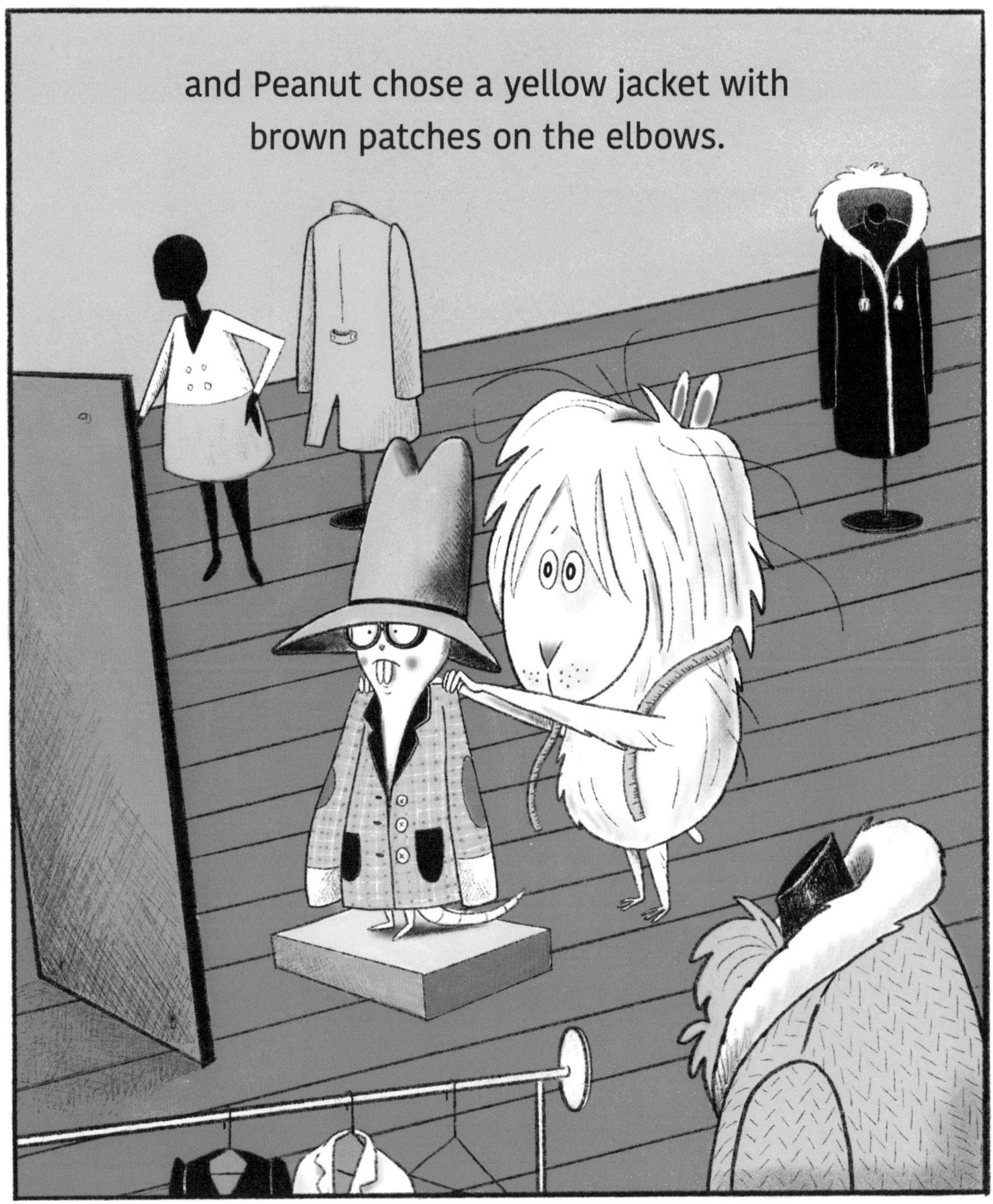

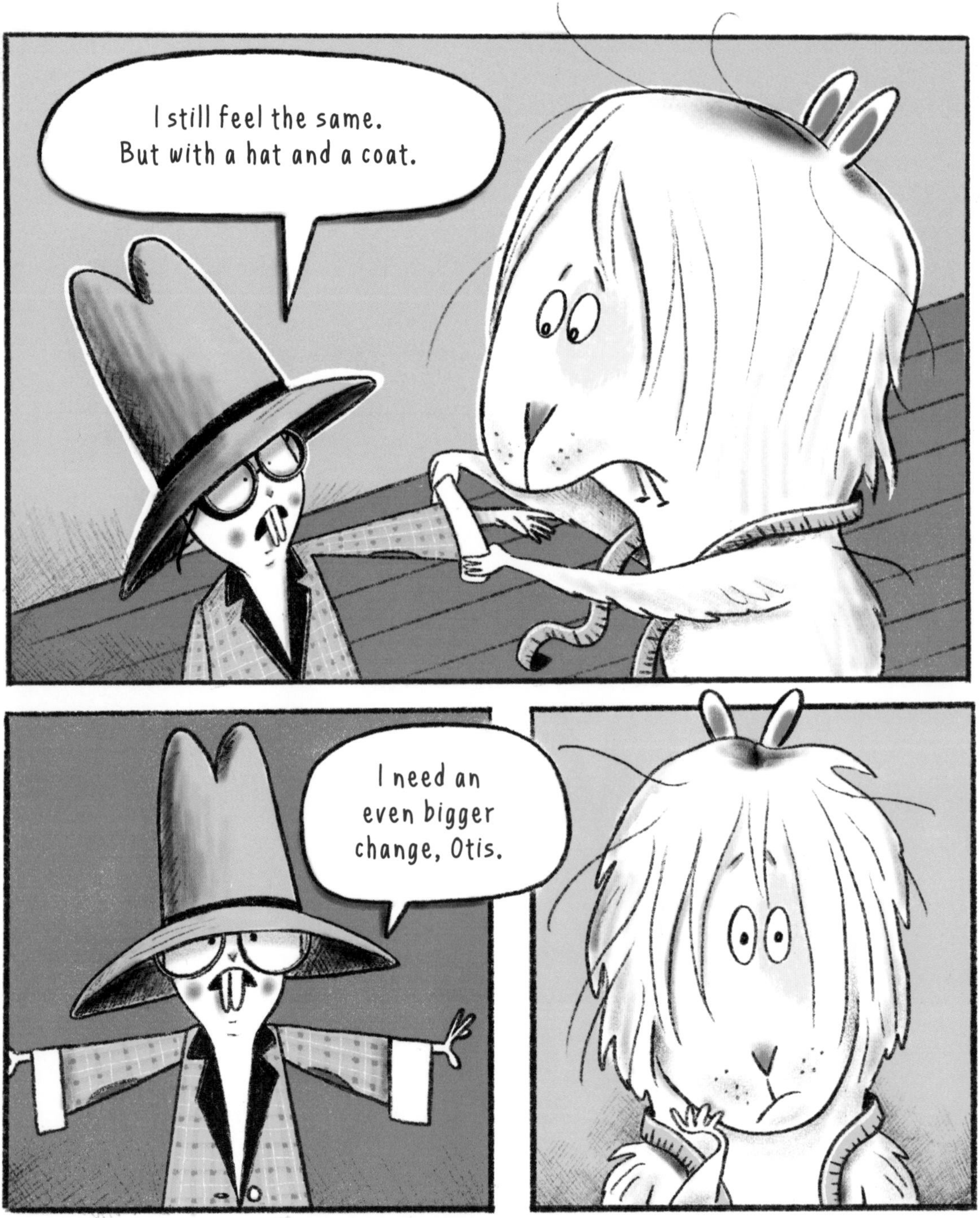
I still feel the same. But with a hat and a coat.
I need an even bigger change, Otis.

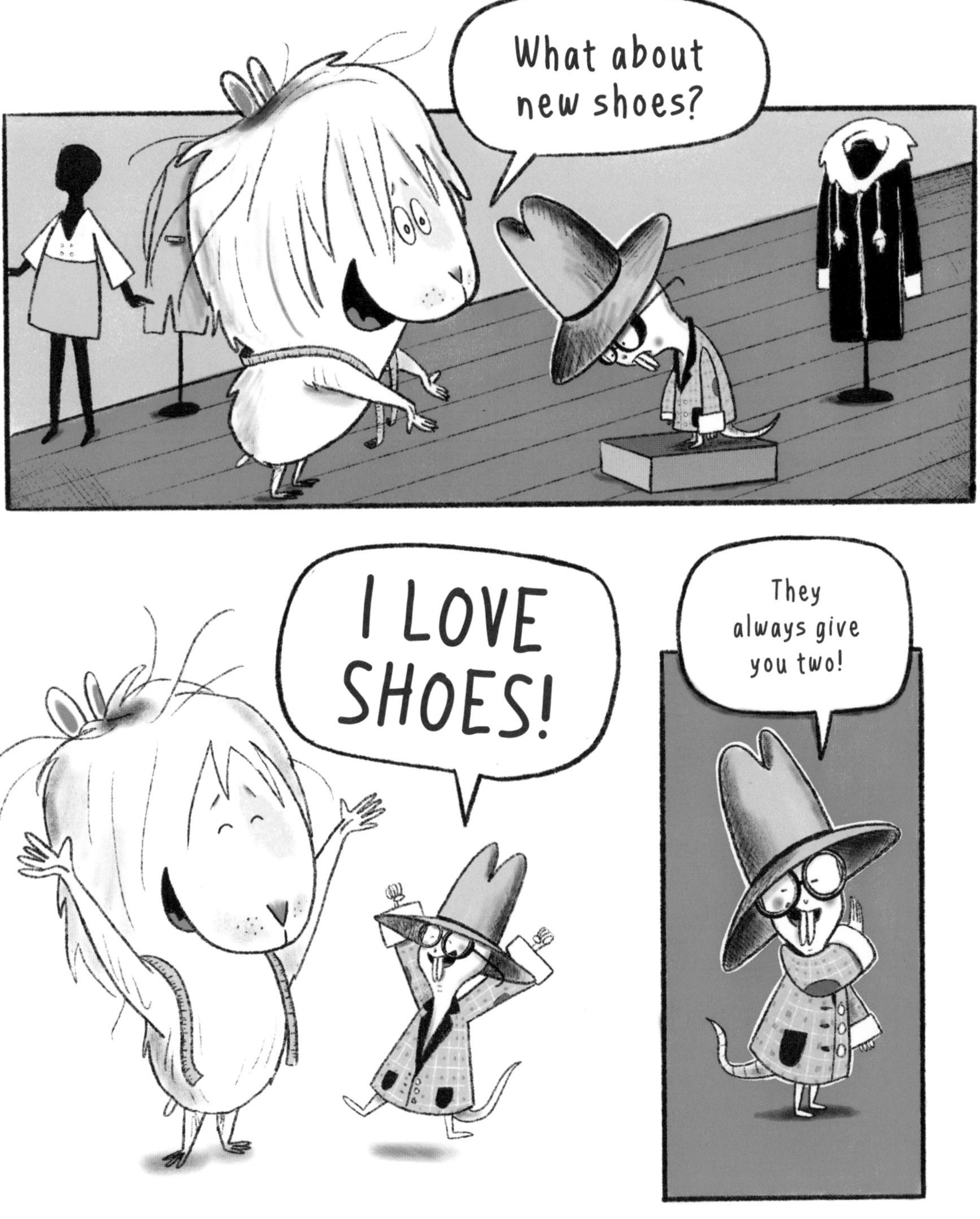
What about new shoes?
I LOVE SHOES!
They always give you two!

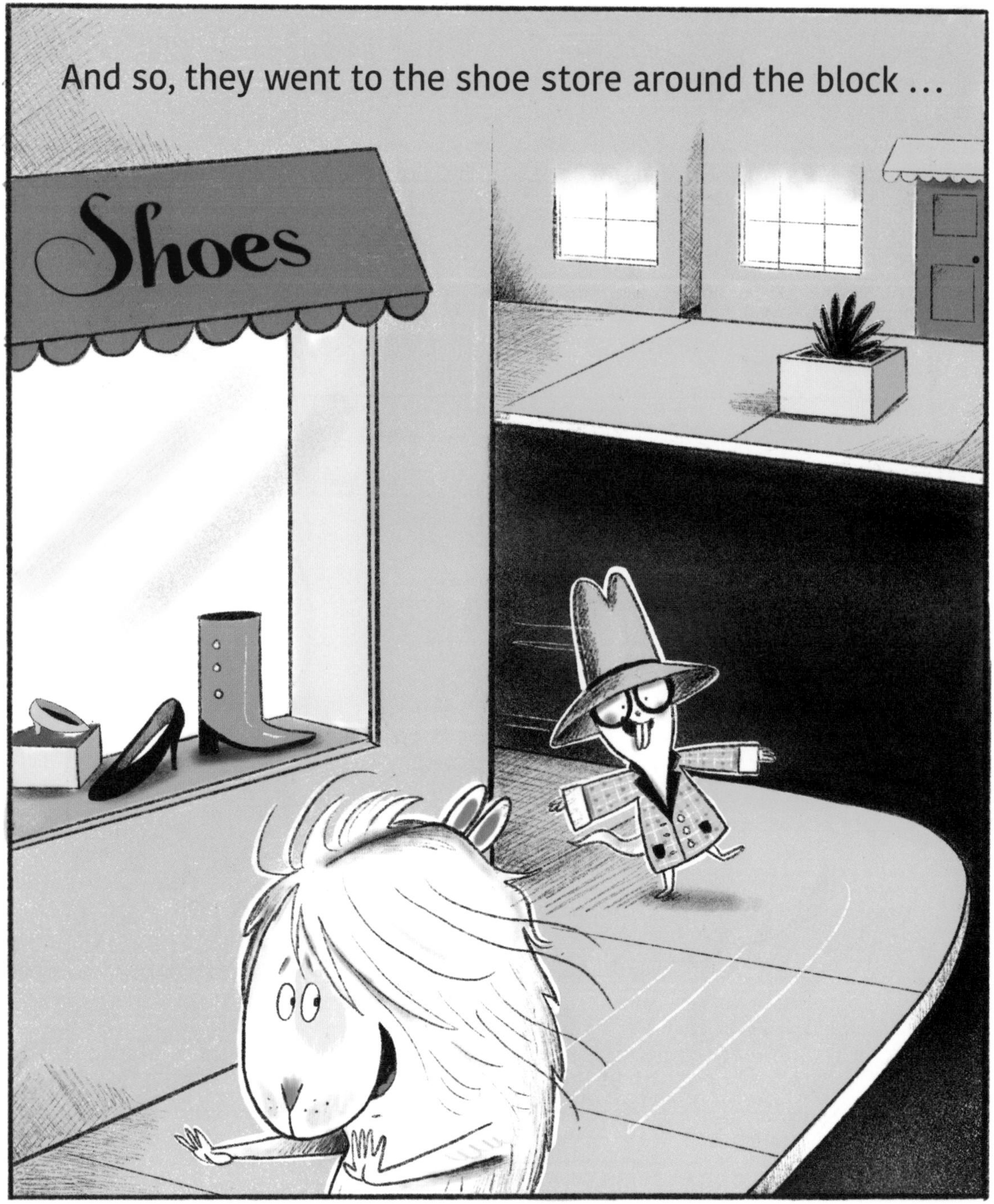
And so, they went to the shoe store around the block ...
Shoes

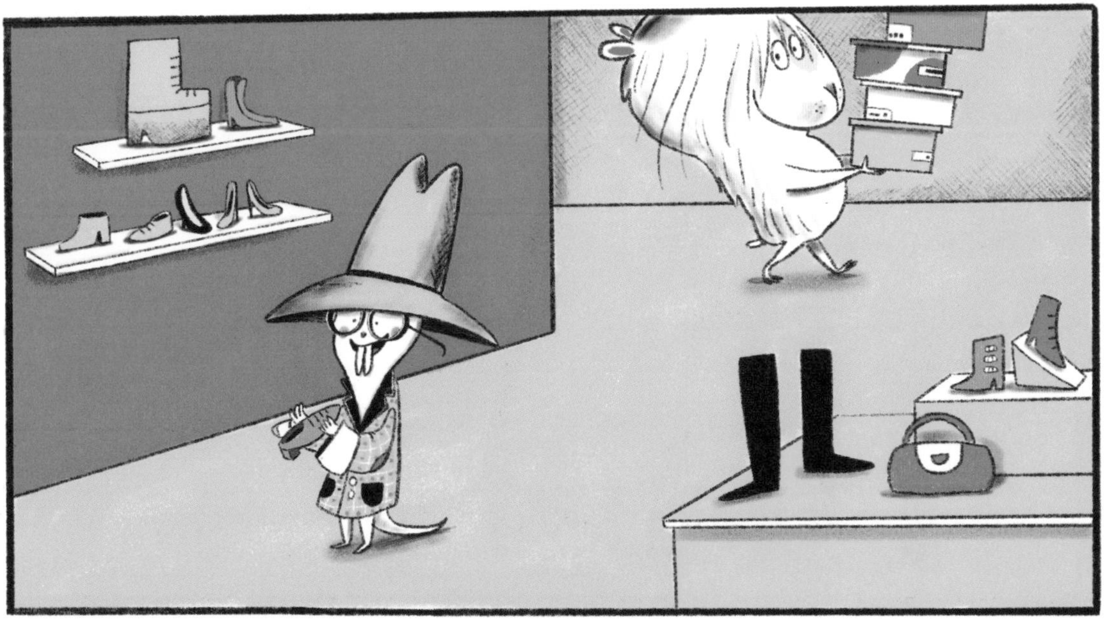

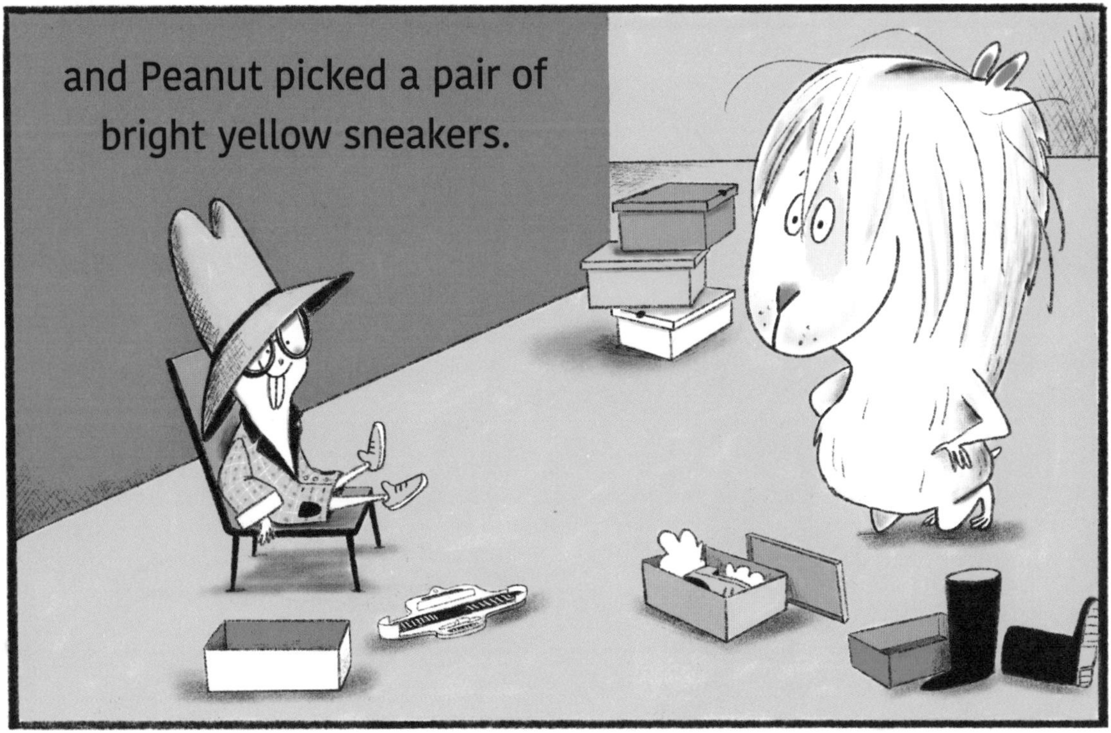
and Peanut picked a pair of bright yellow sneakers.

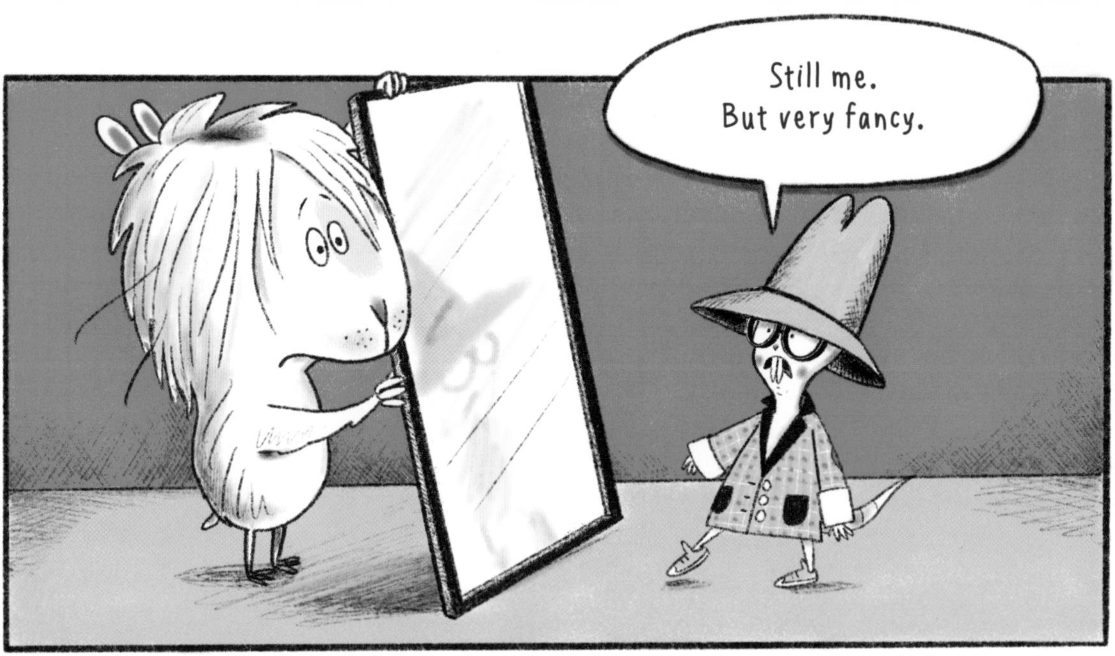
Still me.
But very fancy.

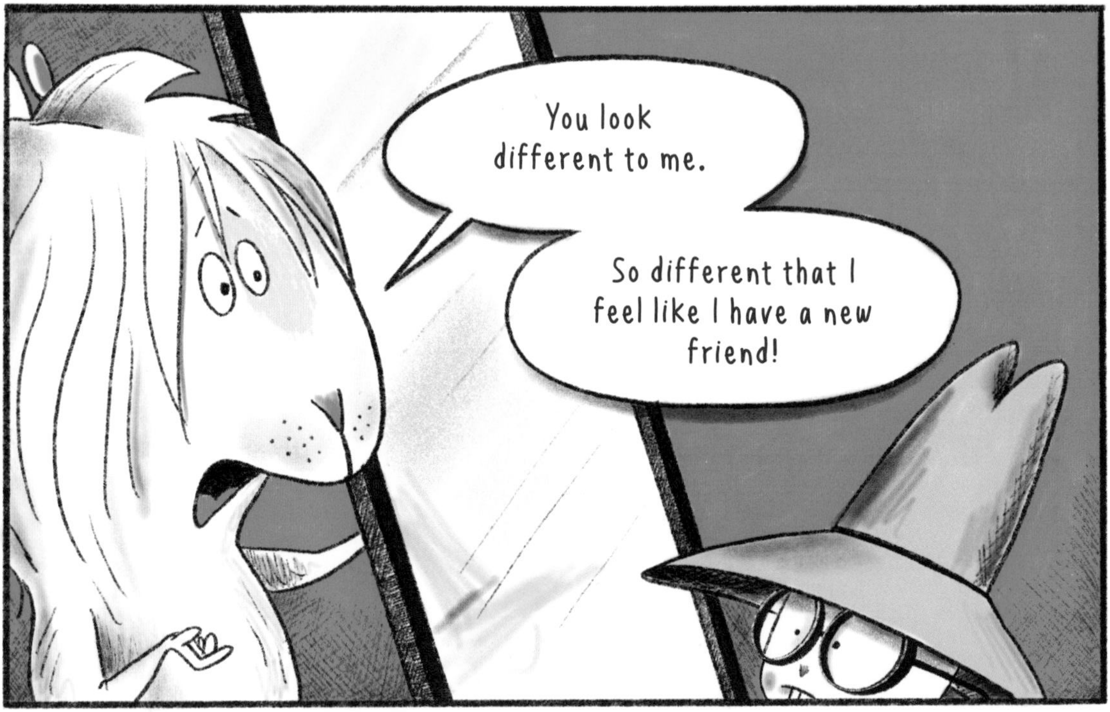
You look different to me.
So different that I feel like I have a new friend!

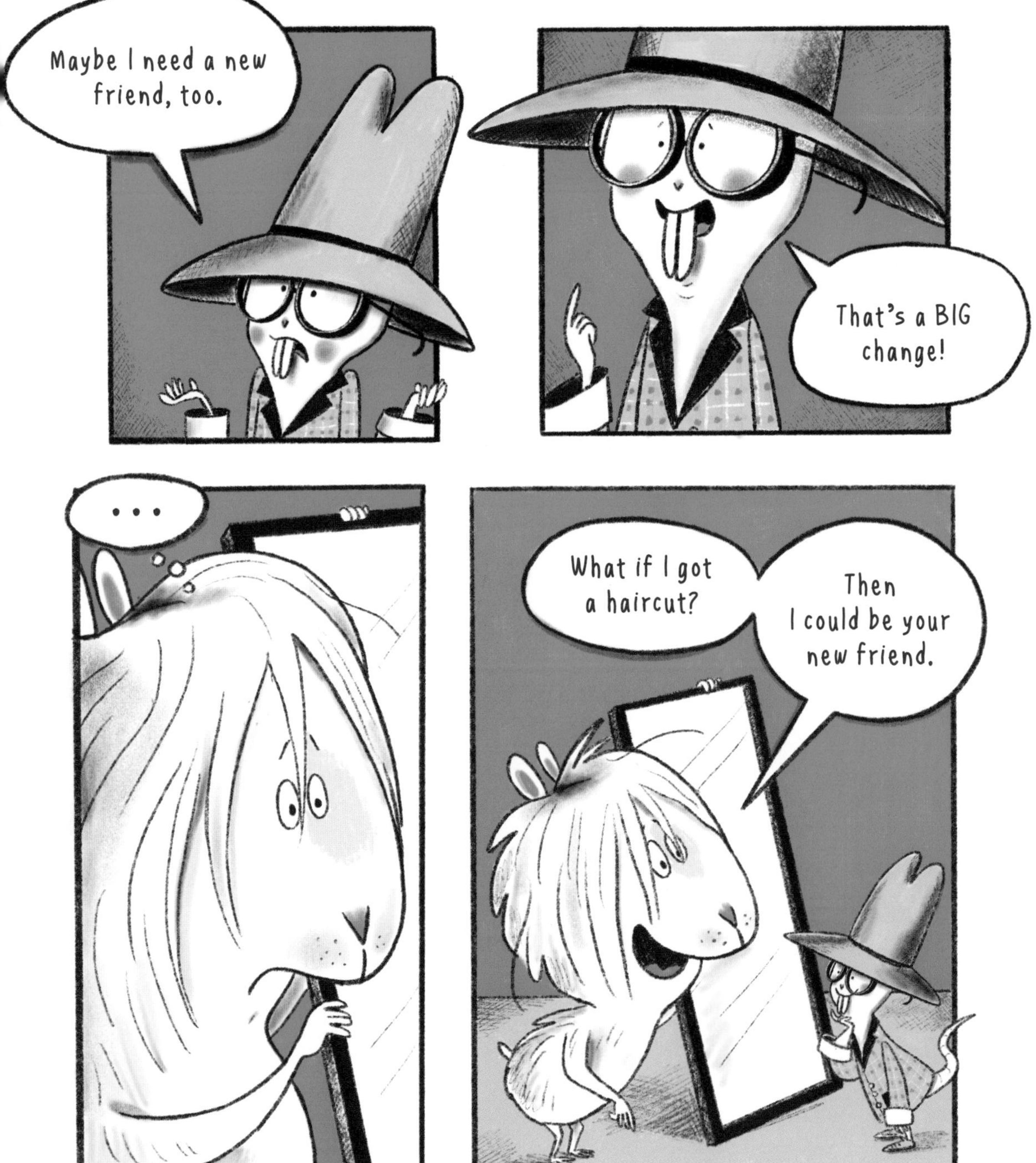
Maybe I need a new friend, too.
That's a BIG change!
...
What if I got a haircut?
Then I could be your new friend.

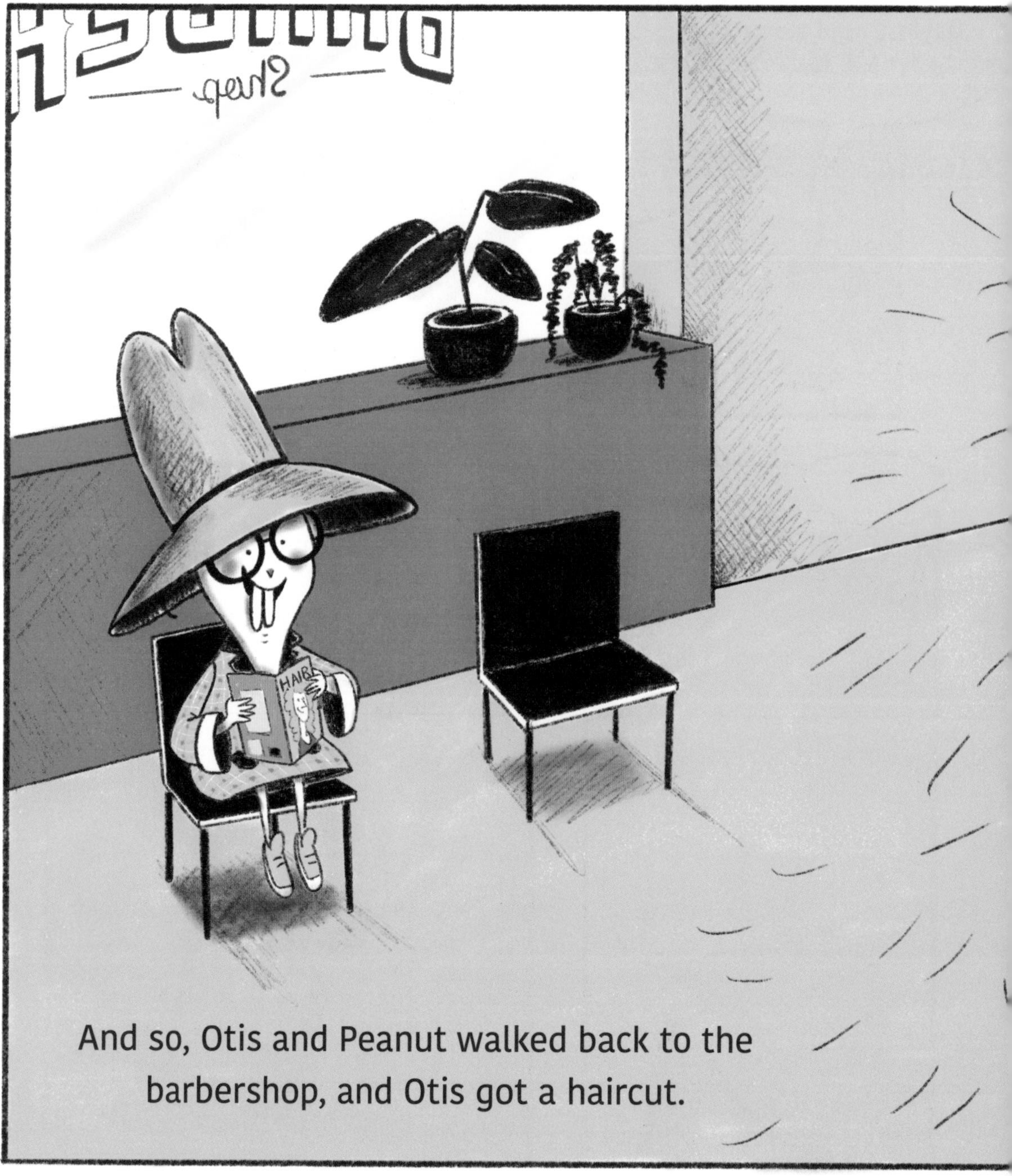

And so, Otis and Peanut walked back to the barbershop, and Otis got a haircut.

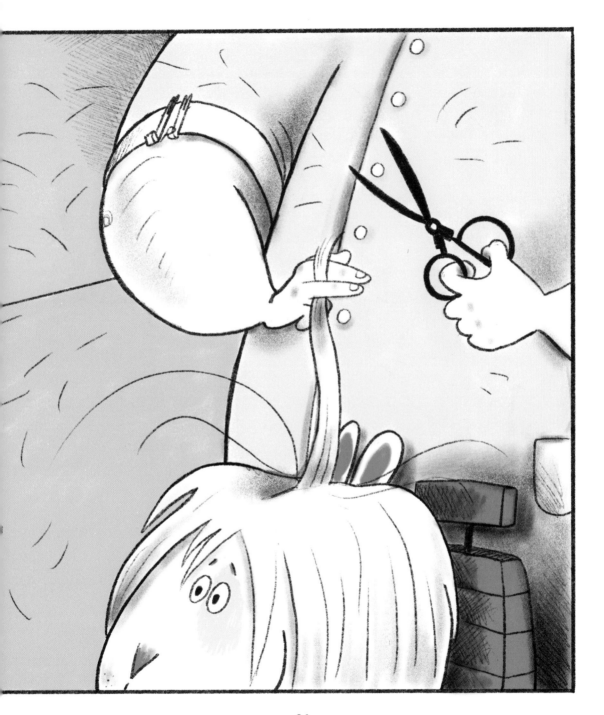

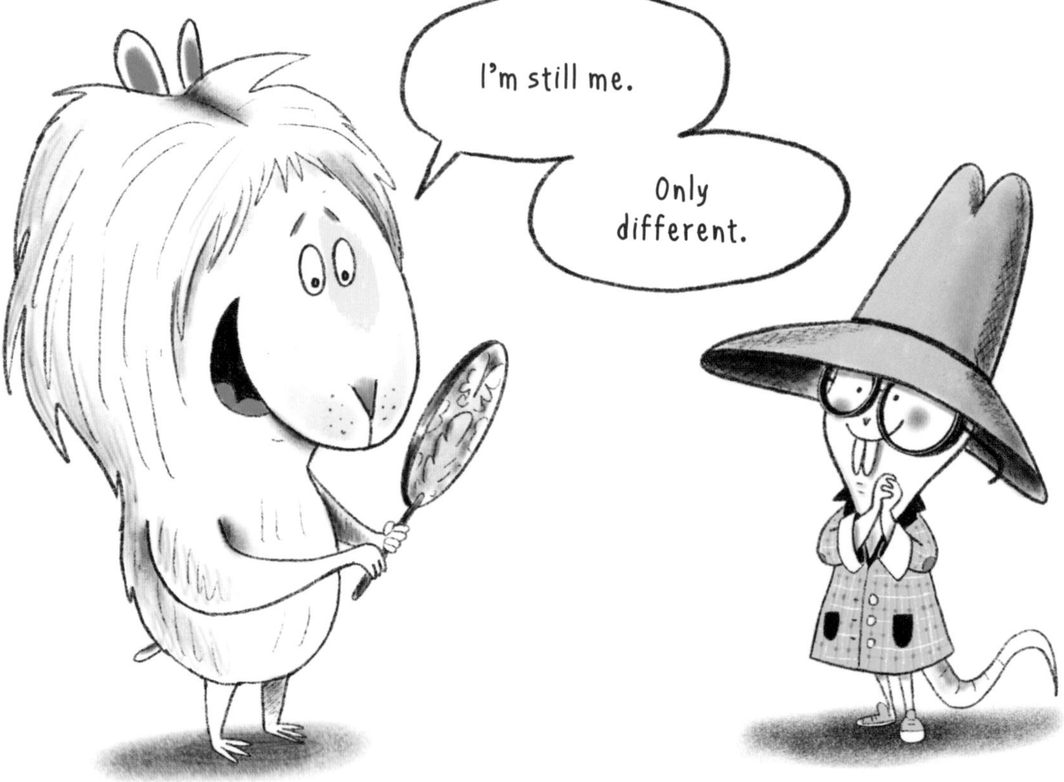
I'm still me.
Only different.

They were both very happy to see a new friend.

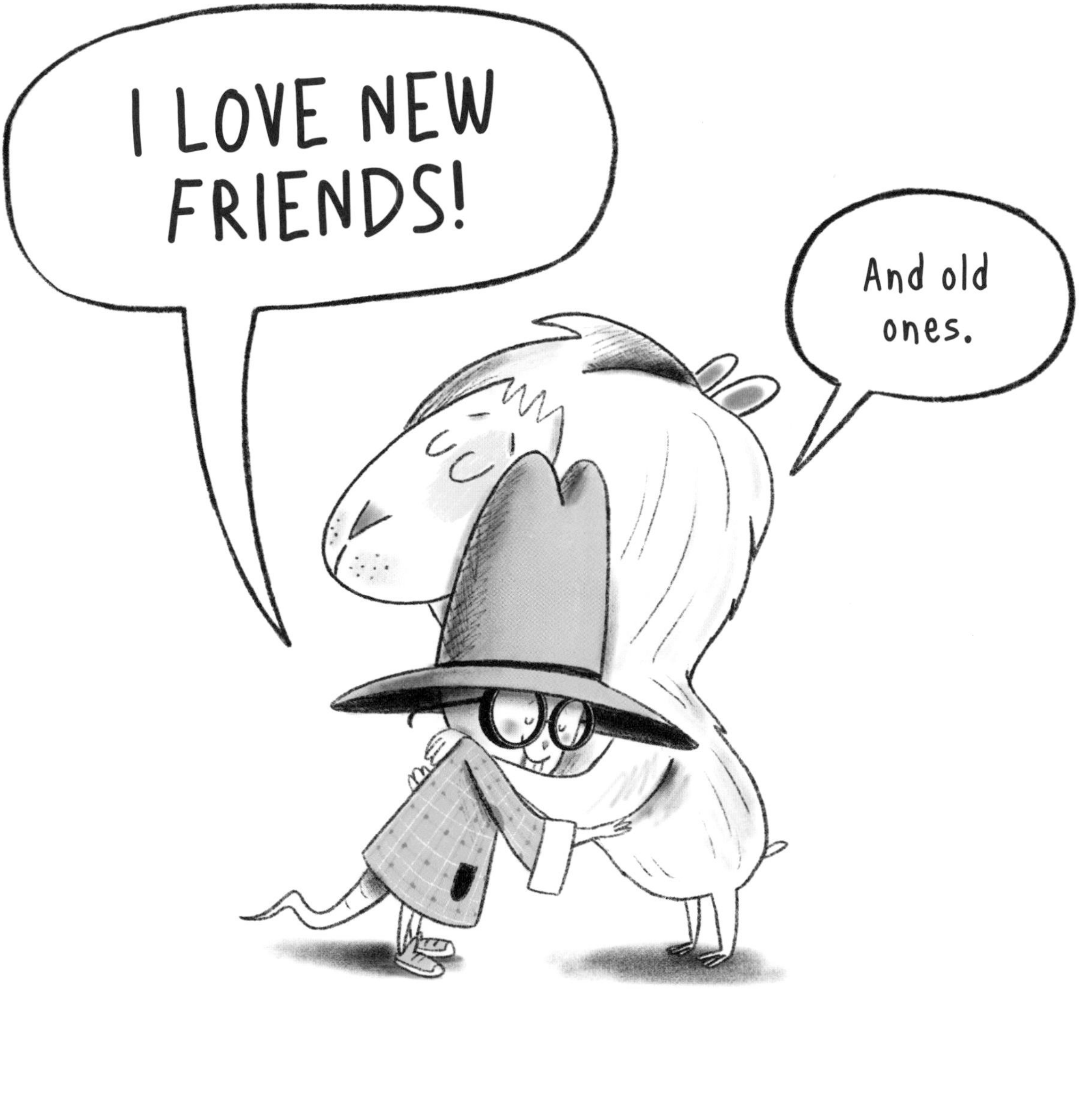
I LOVE NEW FRIENDS!
And old ones.

THE SWING

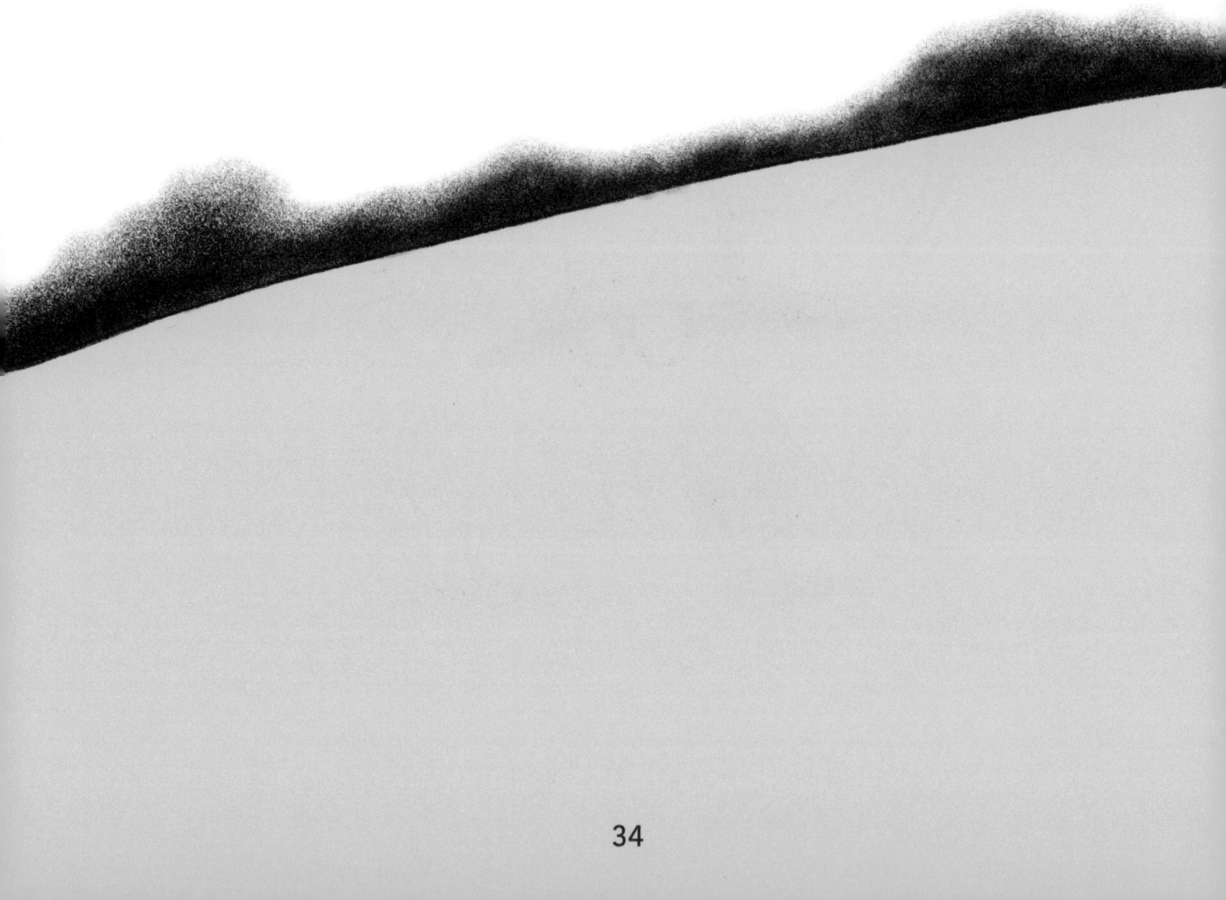

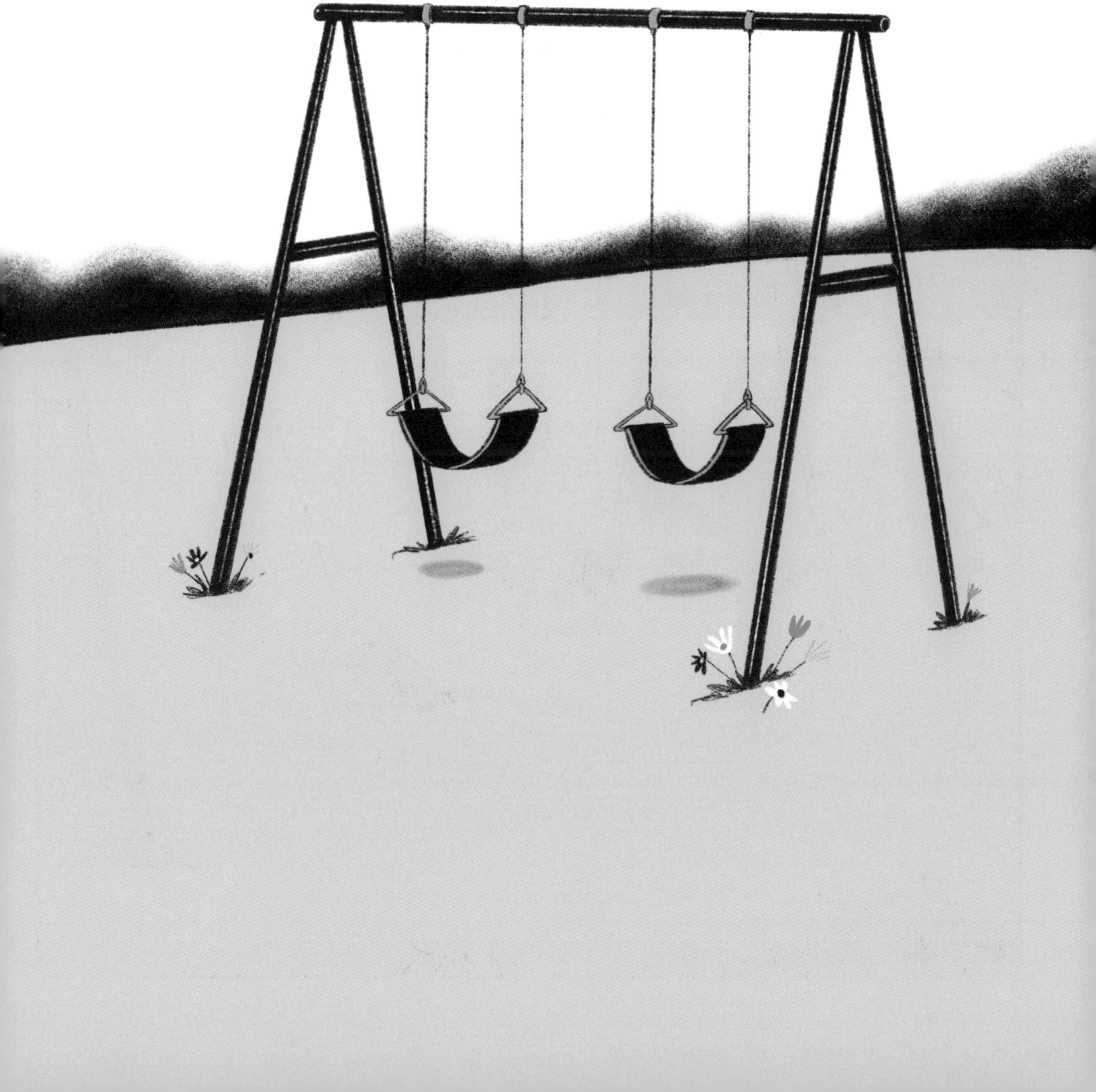

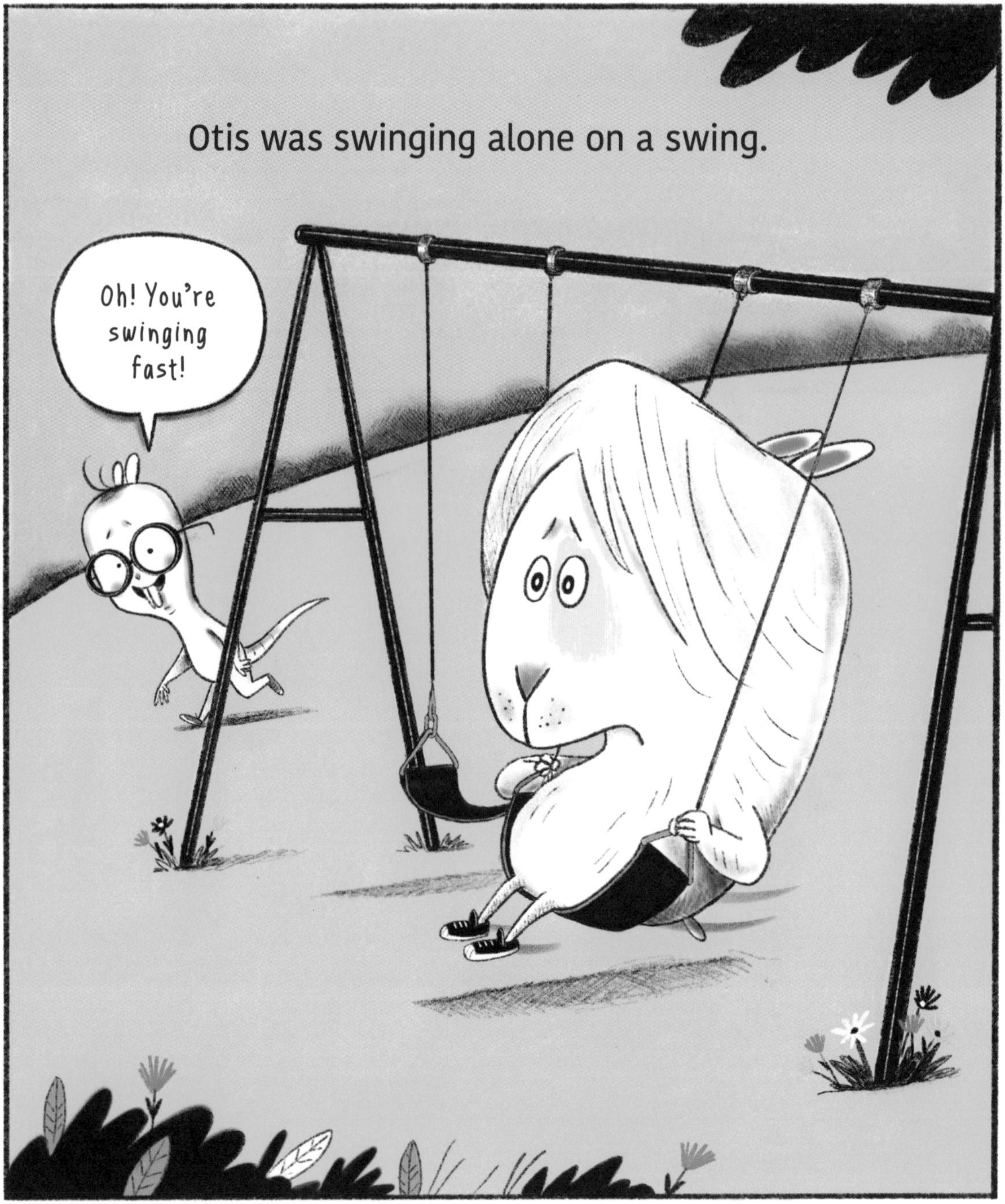
Otis was swinging alone on a swing.
Oh! You're swinging fast!

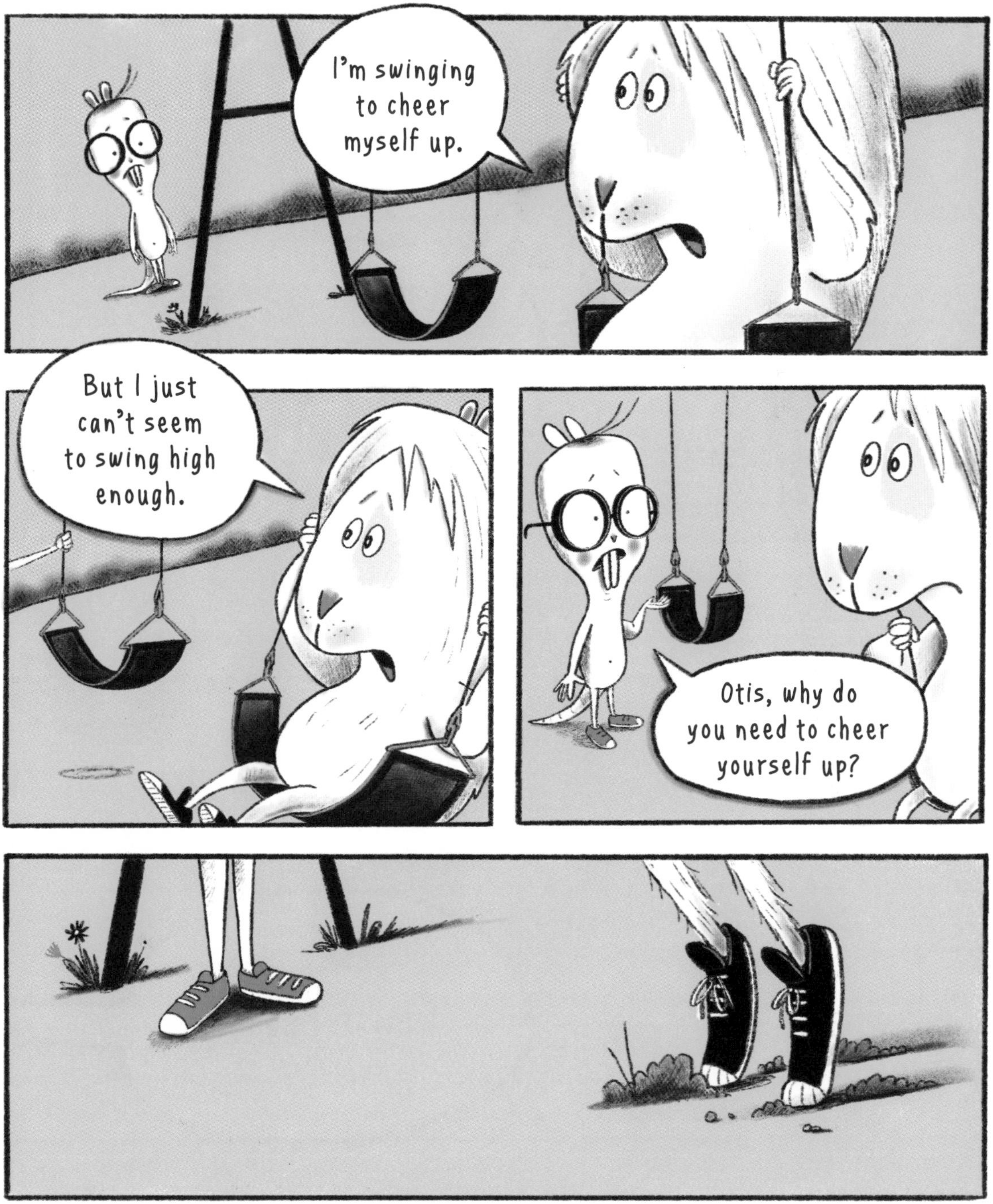
I'm swinging to cheer myself up.
But I just can't seem to swing high enough.
Otis, why do you need to cheer yourself up?

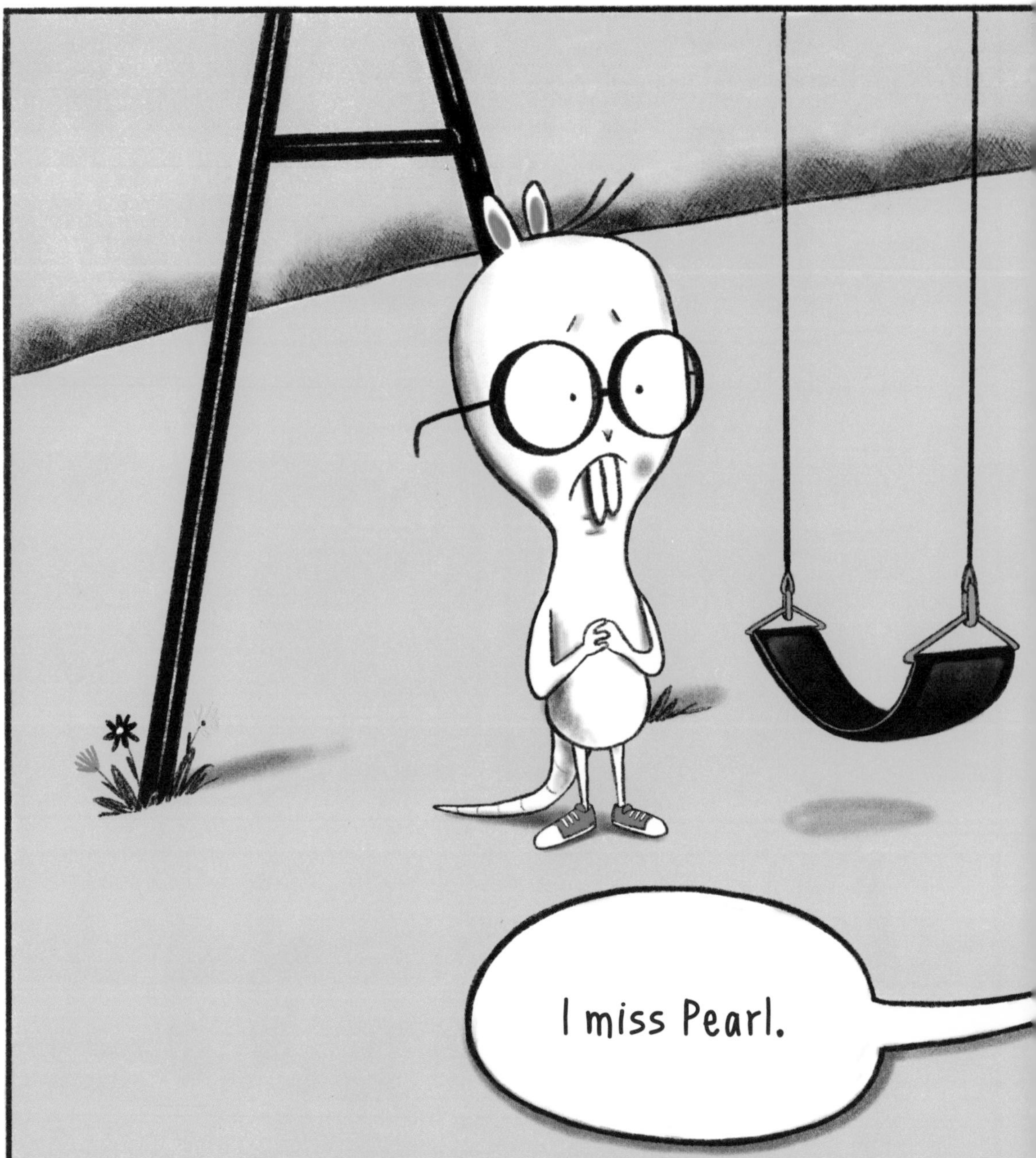
I miss Pearl.

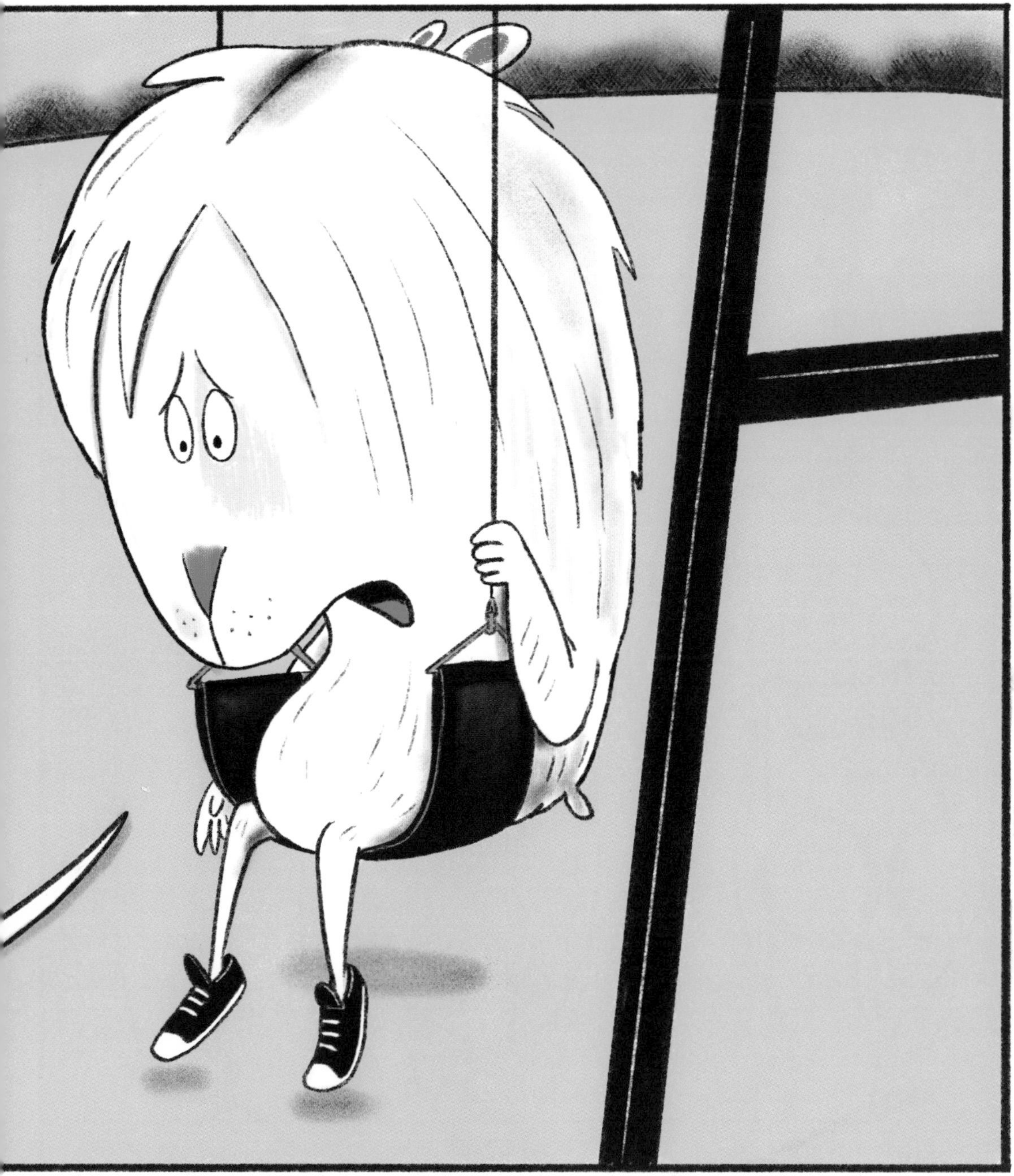

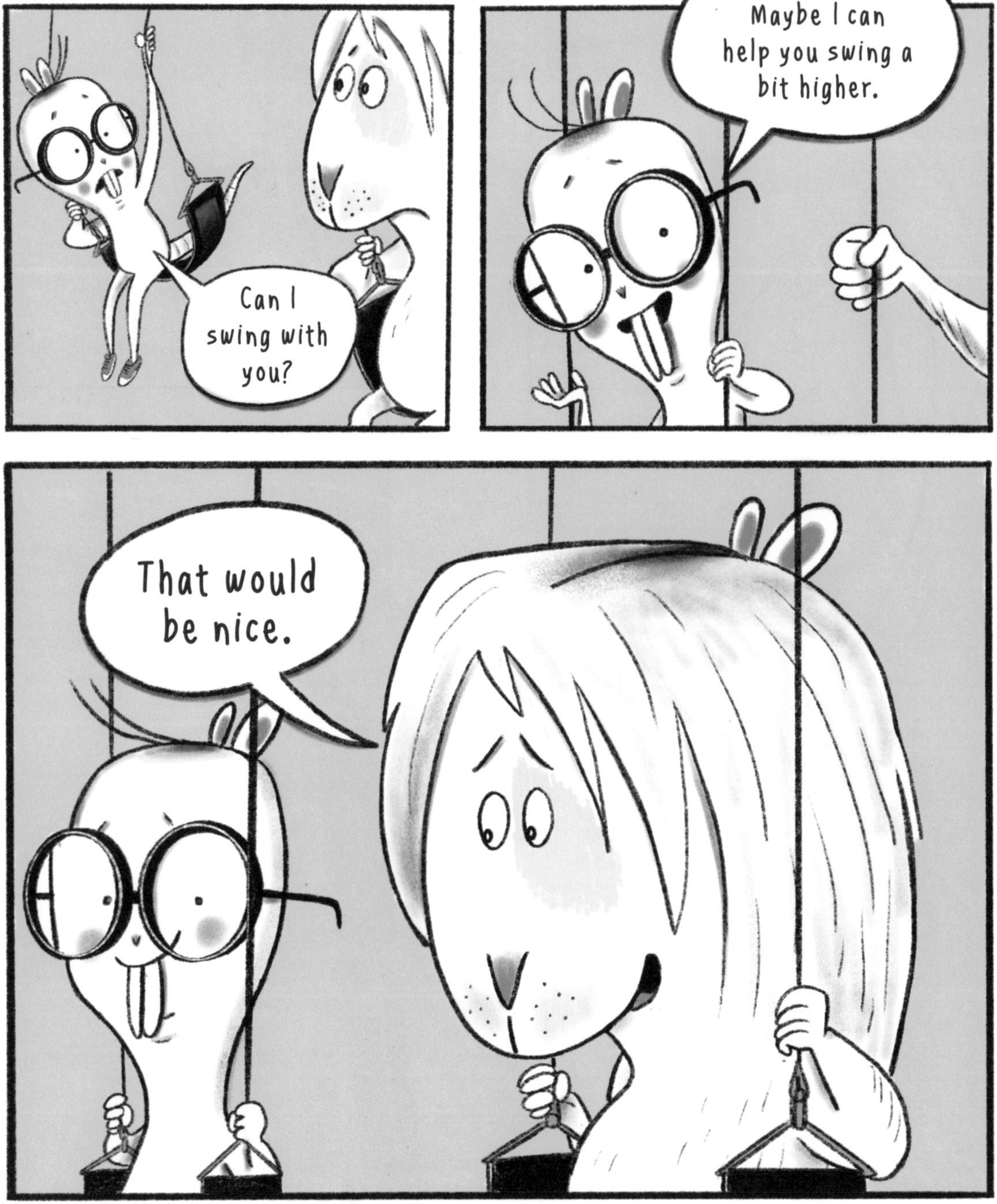
Can I swing with you?
Maybe I can help you swing a bit higher.
That would be nice.

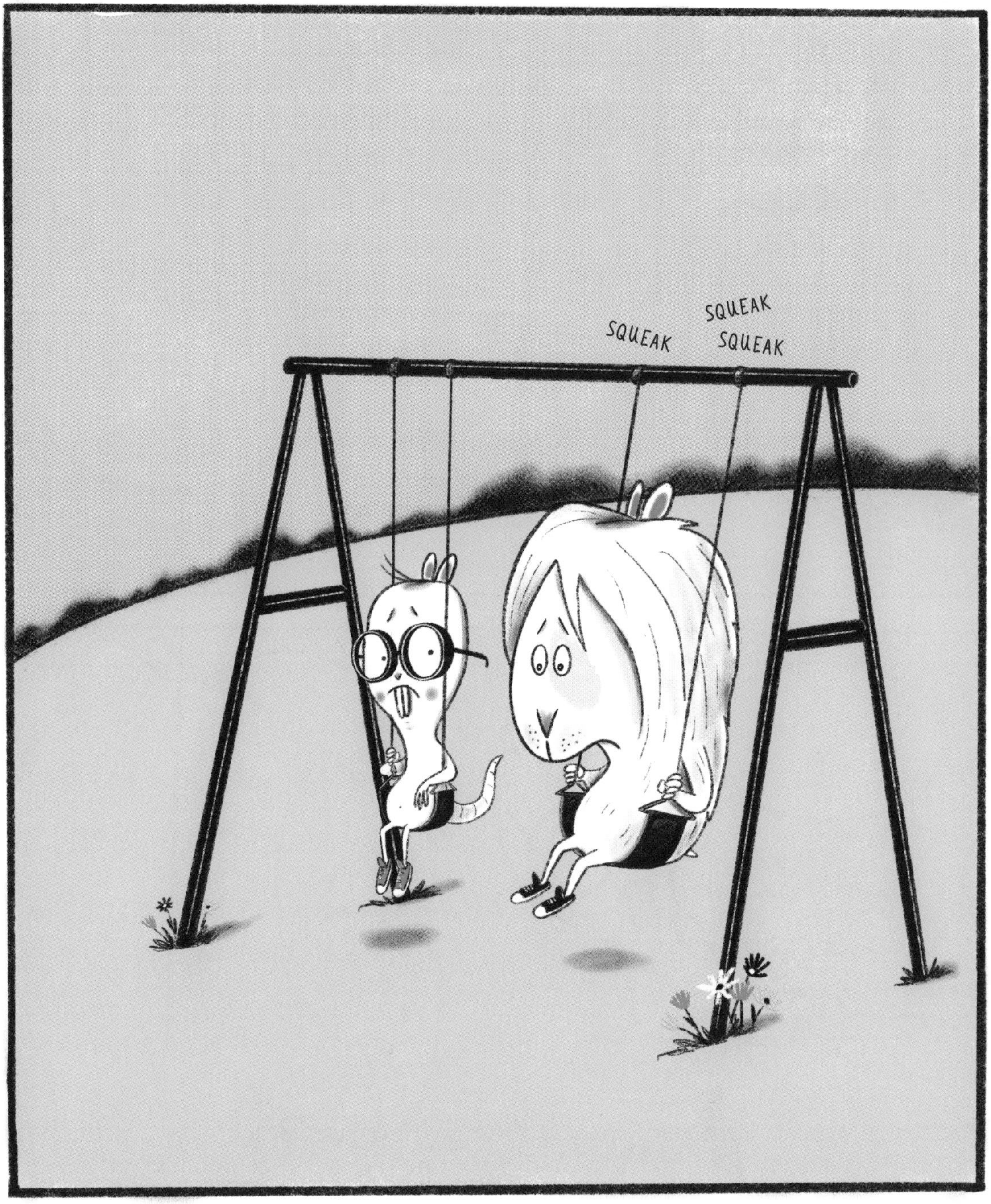
SQUEAK
SQUEAK
SQUEAK

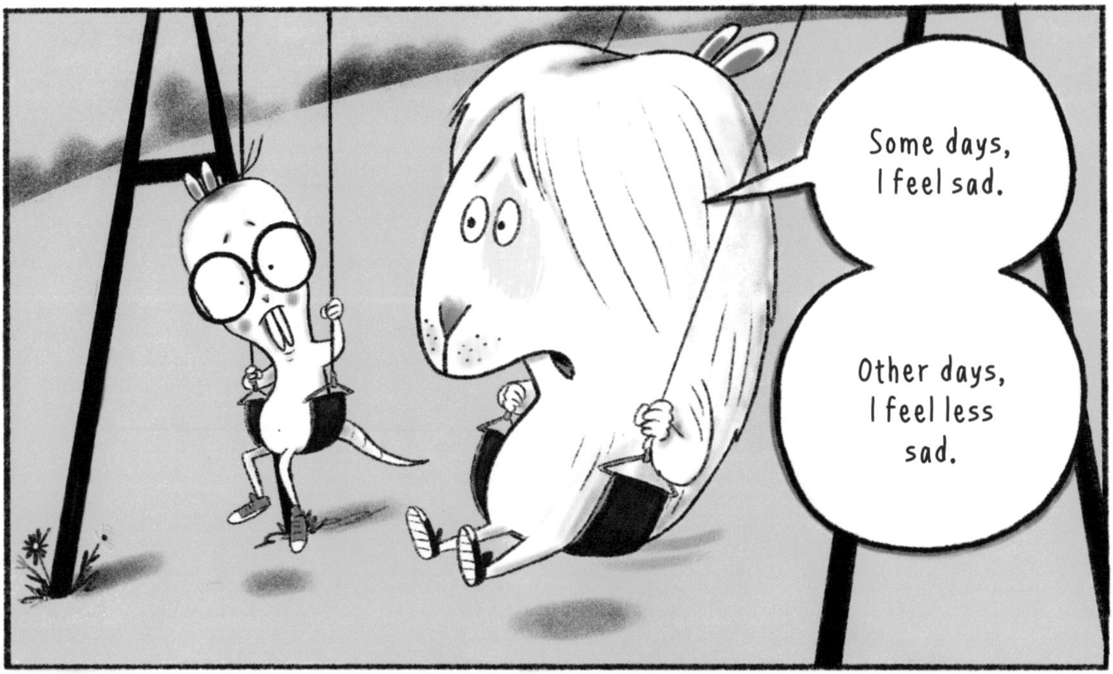
Some days, I feel sad.
Other days, I feel less sad.

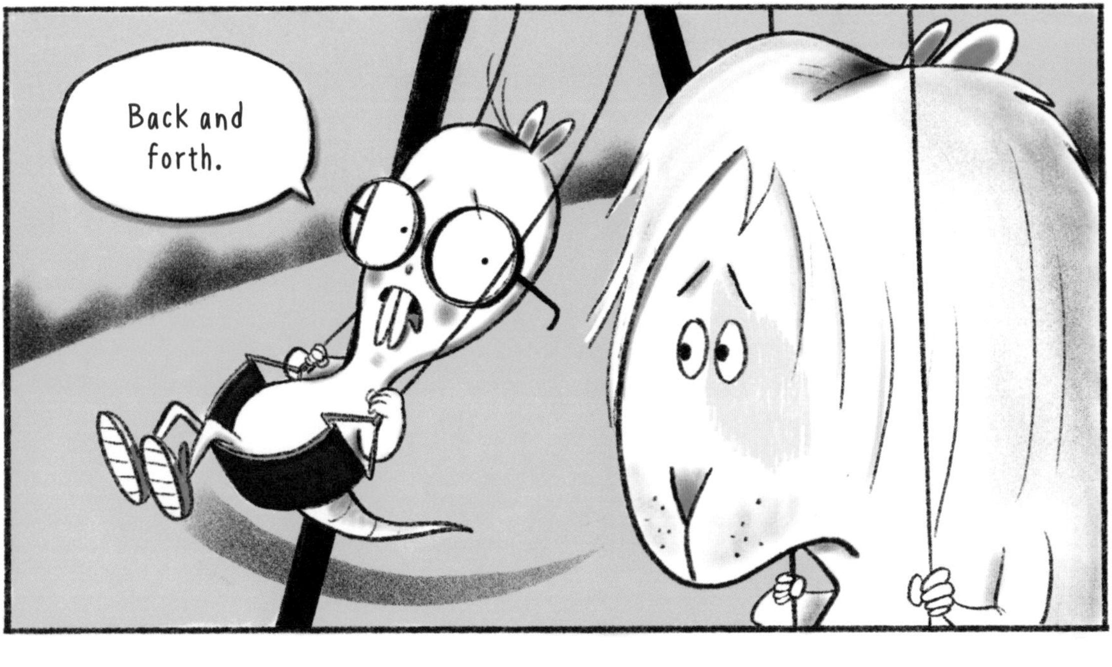
Back and forth.

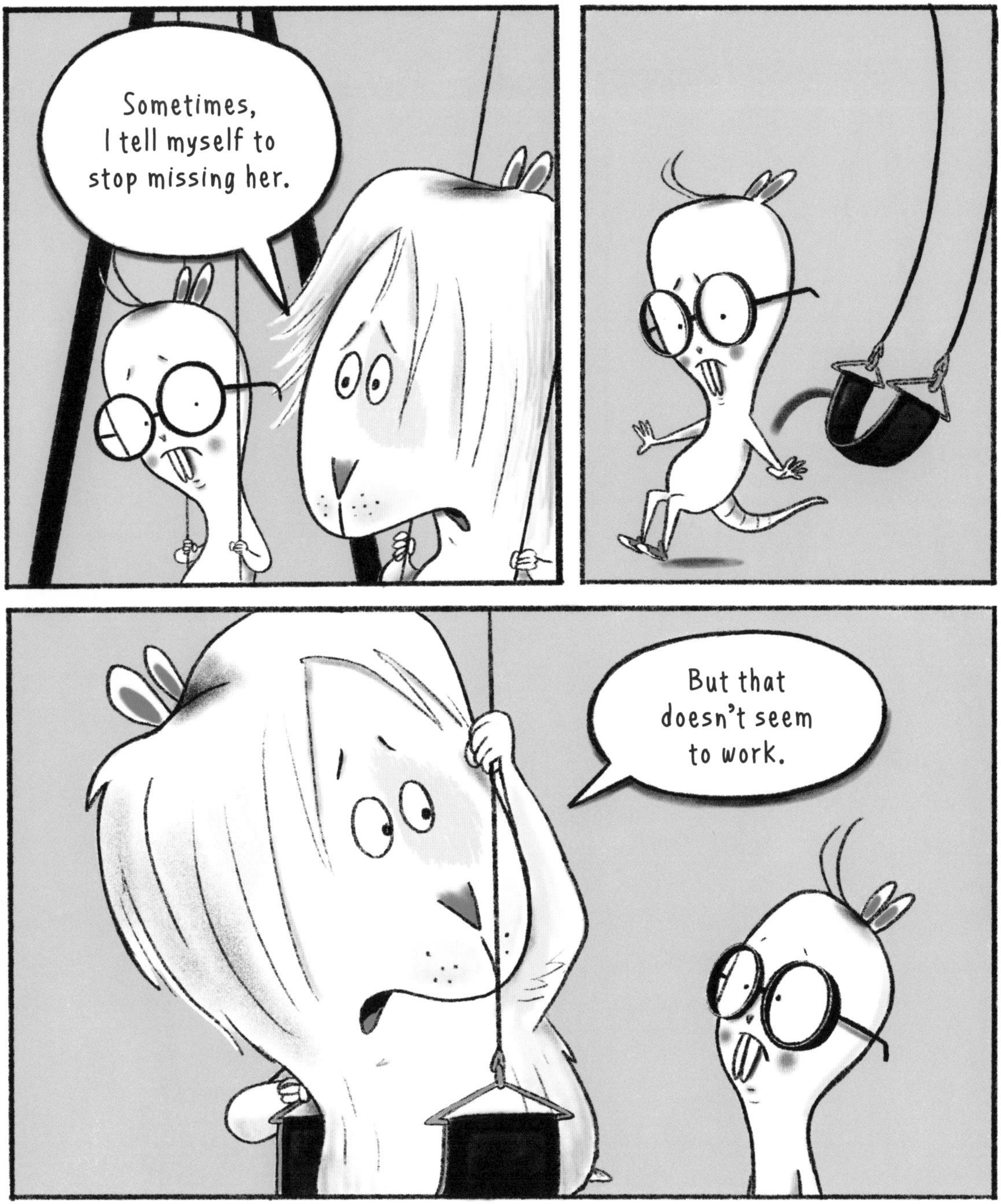
Sometimes, I tell myself to stop missing her.
But that doesn't seem to work.

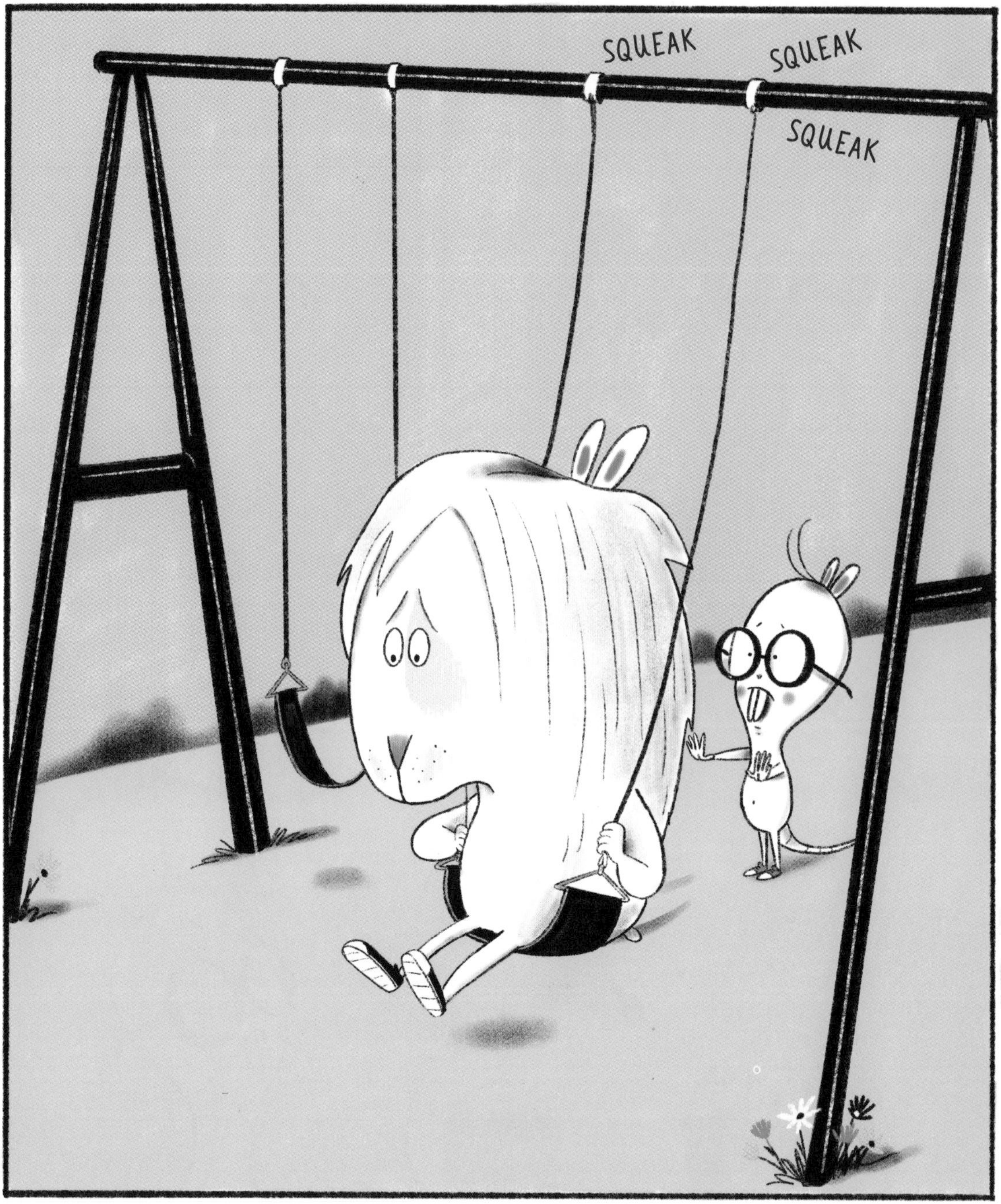
SQUEAK
SQUEAK
SQUEAK

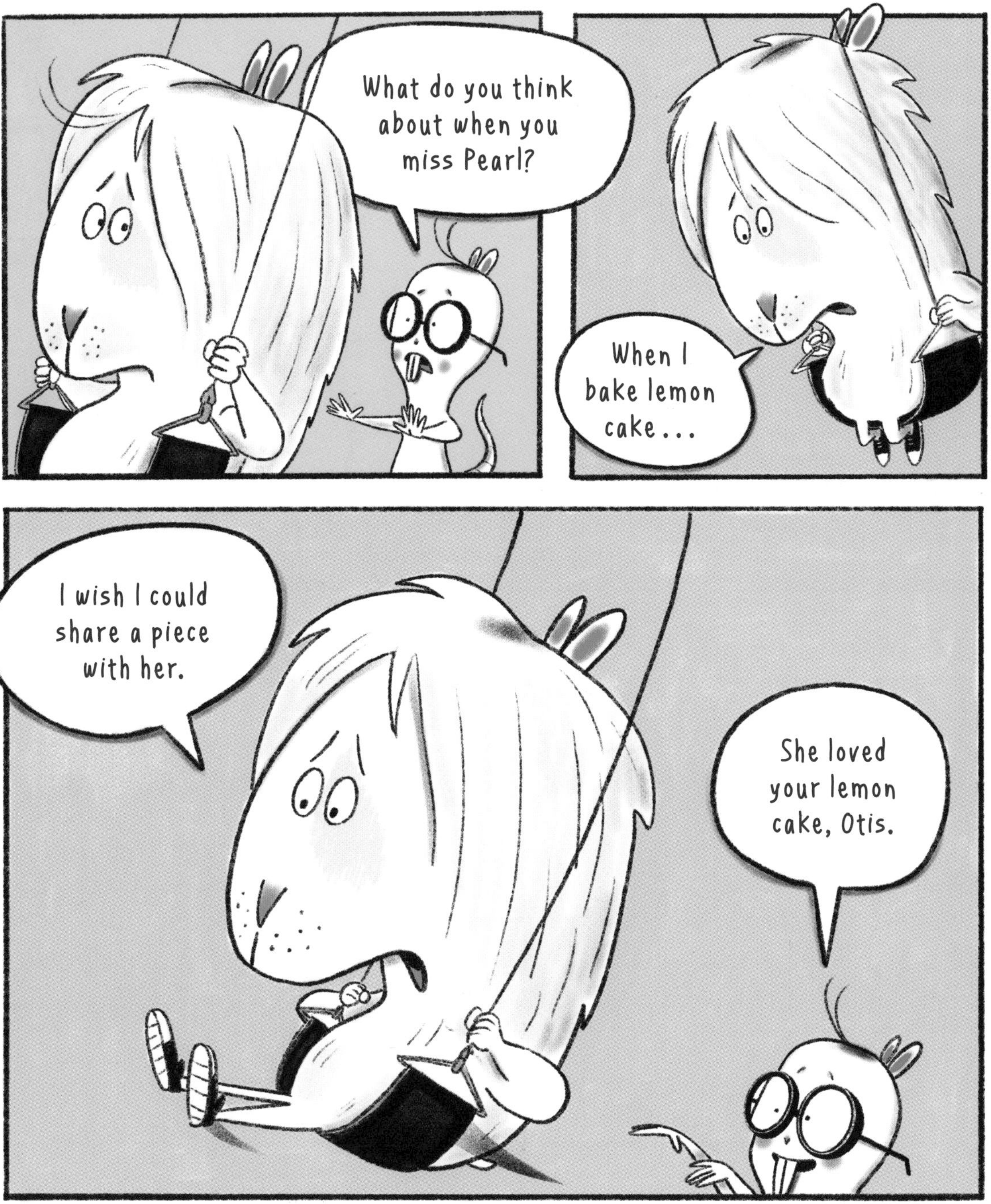
What do you think about when you miss Pearl?
When I bake lemon cake . . .
I wish I could share a piece with her.
She loved your lemon cake, Otis.

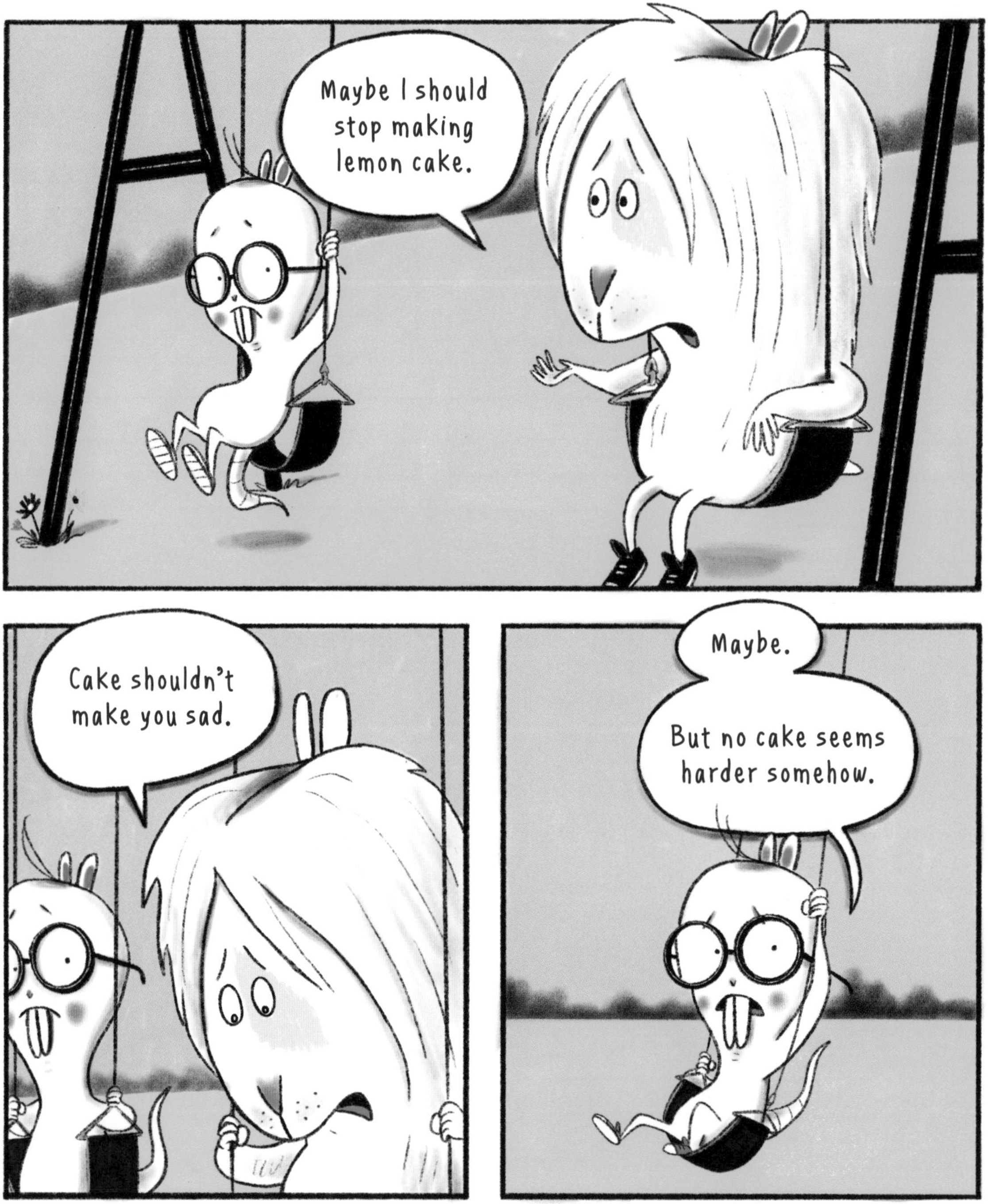
Maybe I should stop making lemon cake.
Cake shouldn't make you sad.
Maybe.
But no cake seems harder somehow.

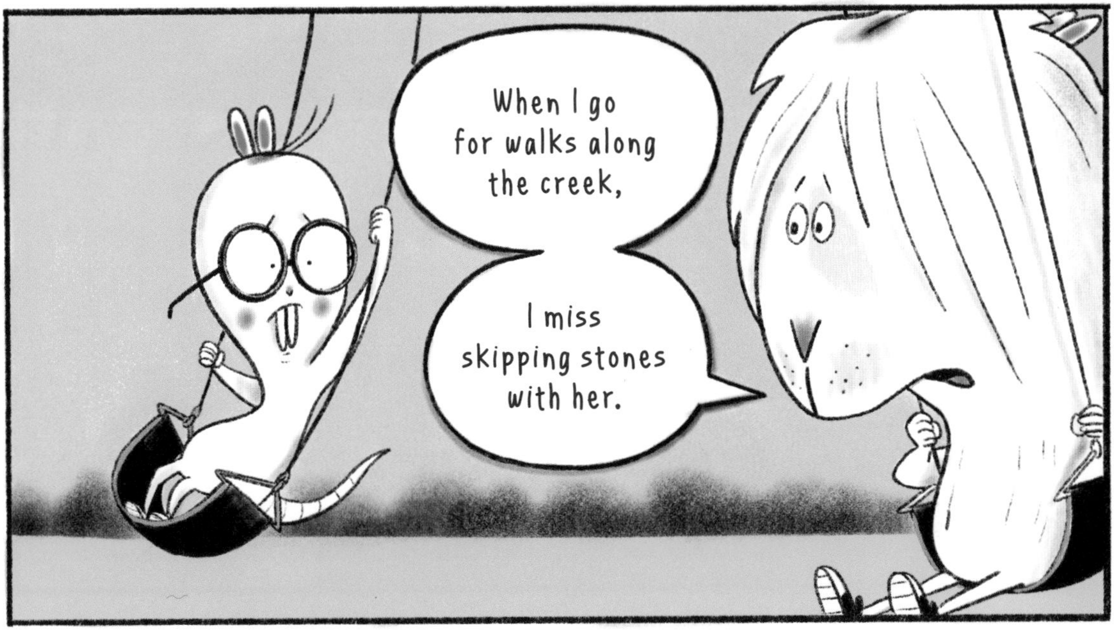
When I go for walks along the creek,
I miss skipping stones with her.

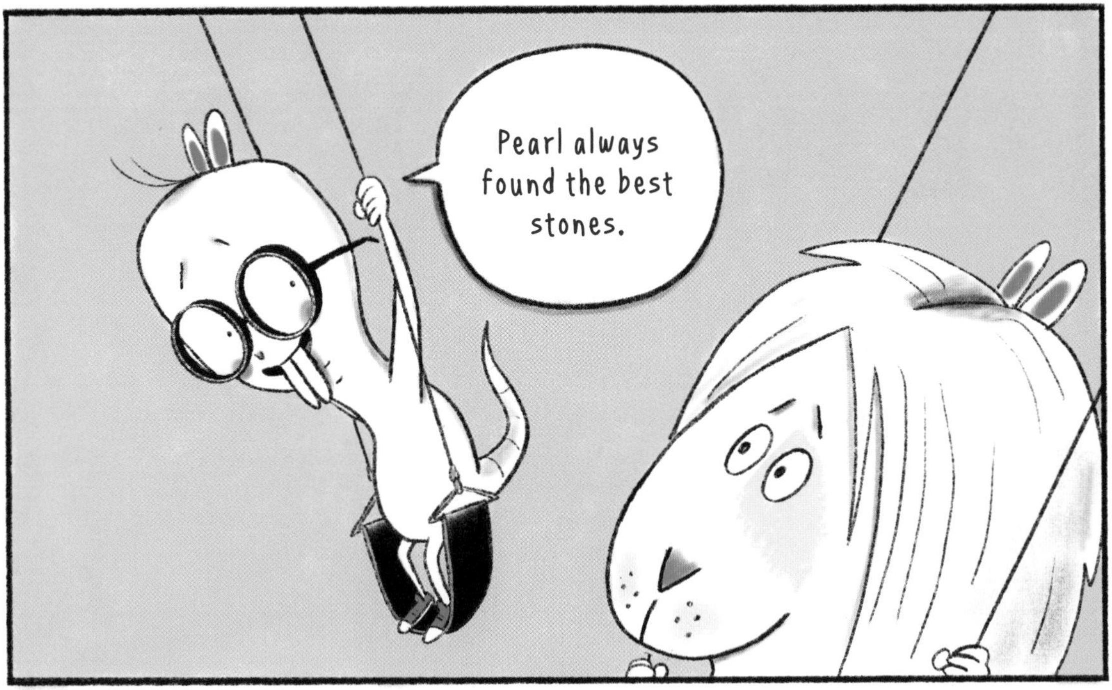
Pearl always found the best stones.

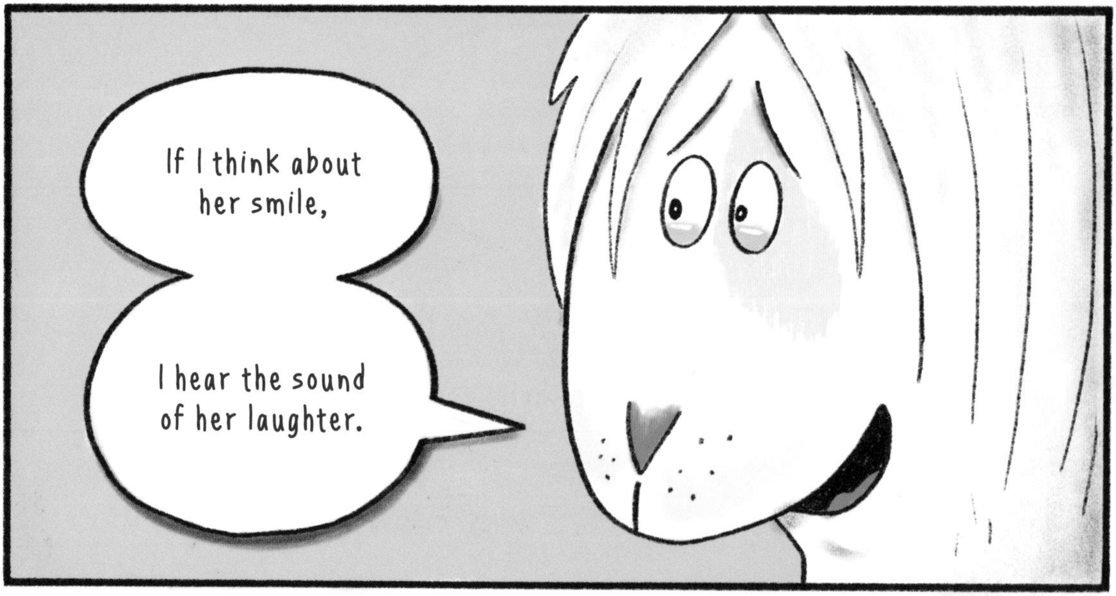
If I think about her smile,
I hear the sound of her laughter.

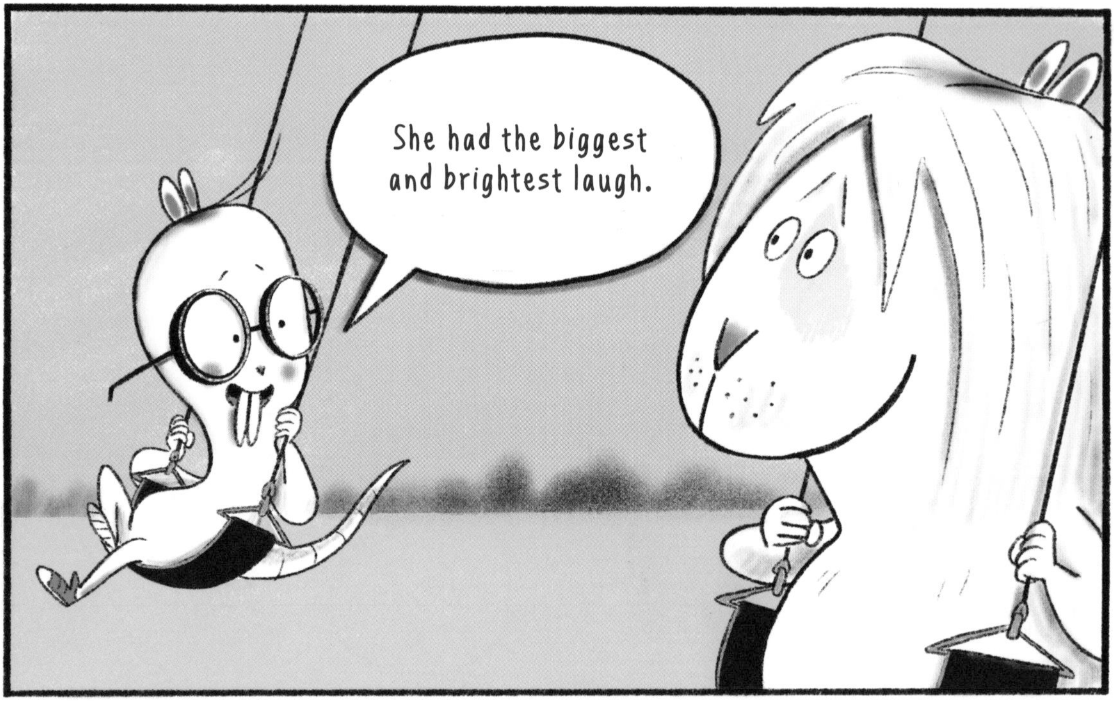
She had the biggest and brightest laugh.

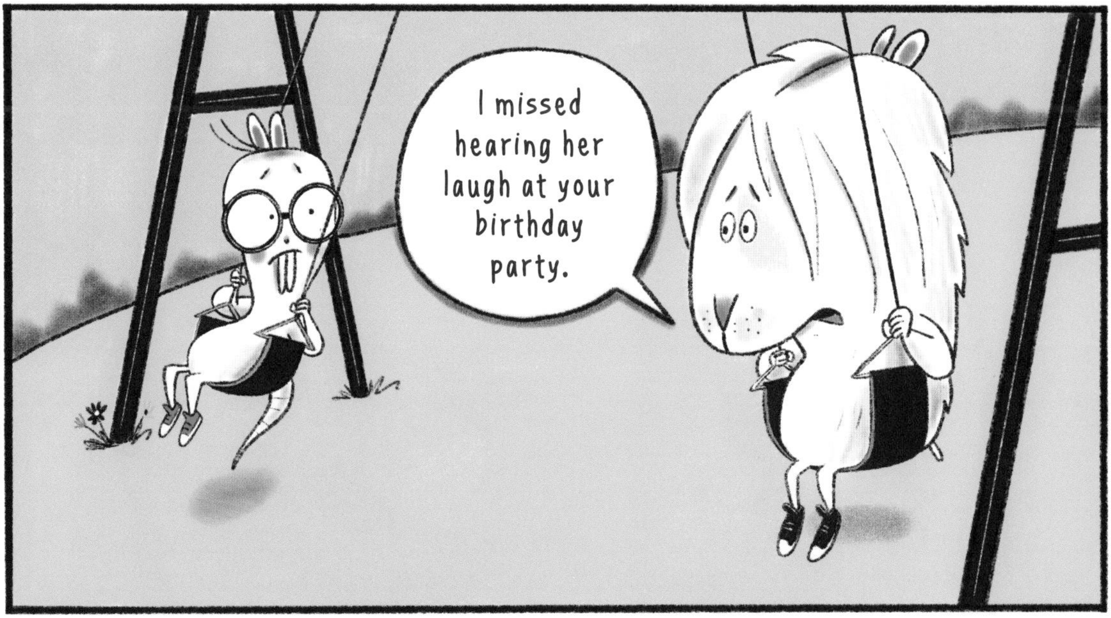
I missed hearing her laugh at your birthday party.

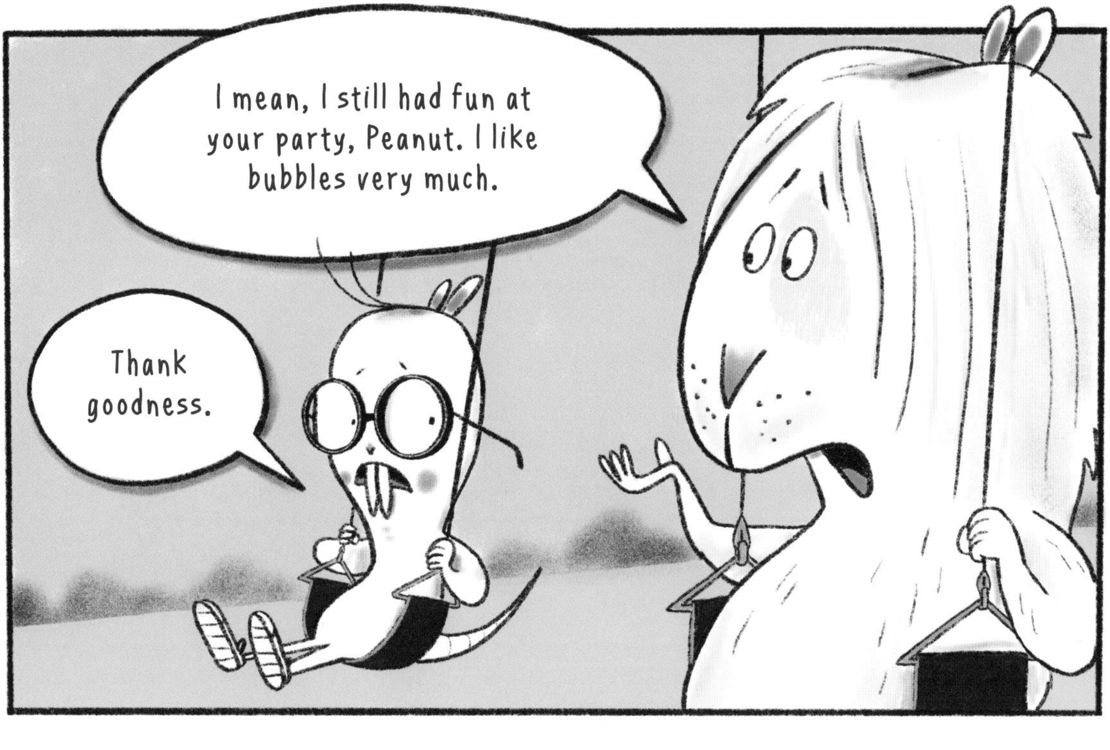
I mean, I still had fun at your party, Peanut. I like bubbles very much.
Thank goodness.

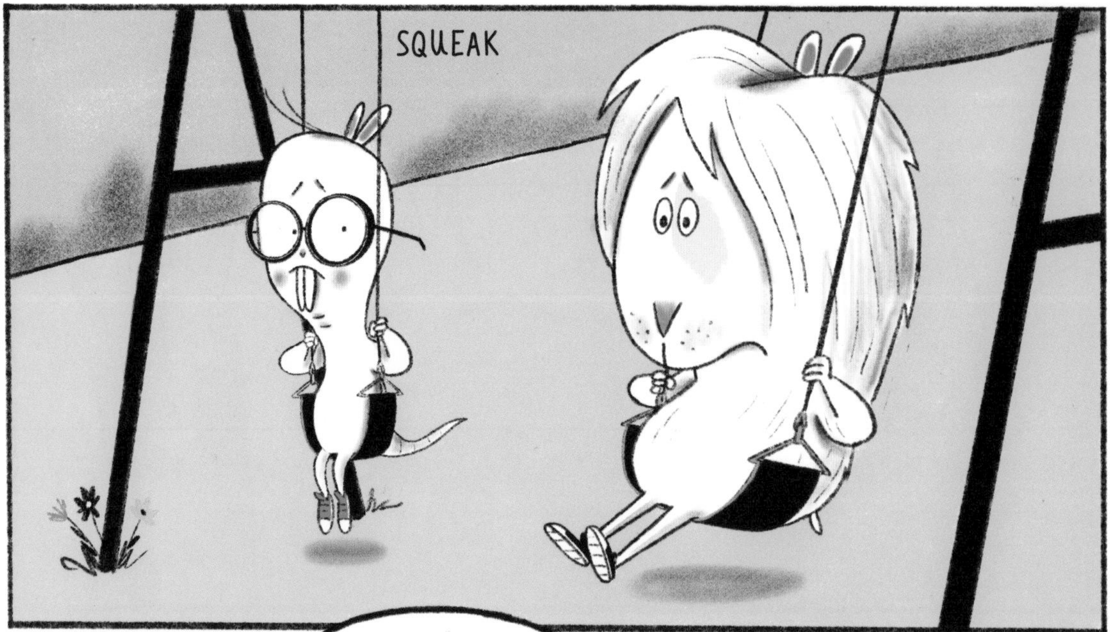
SQUEAK

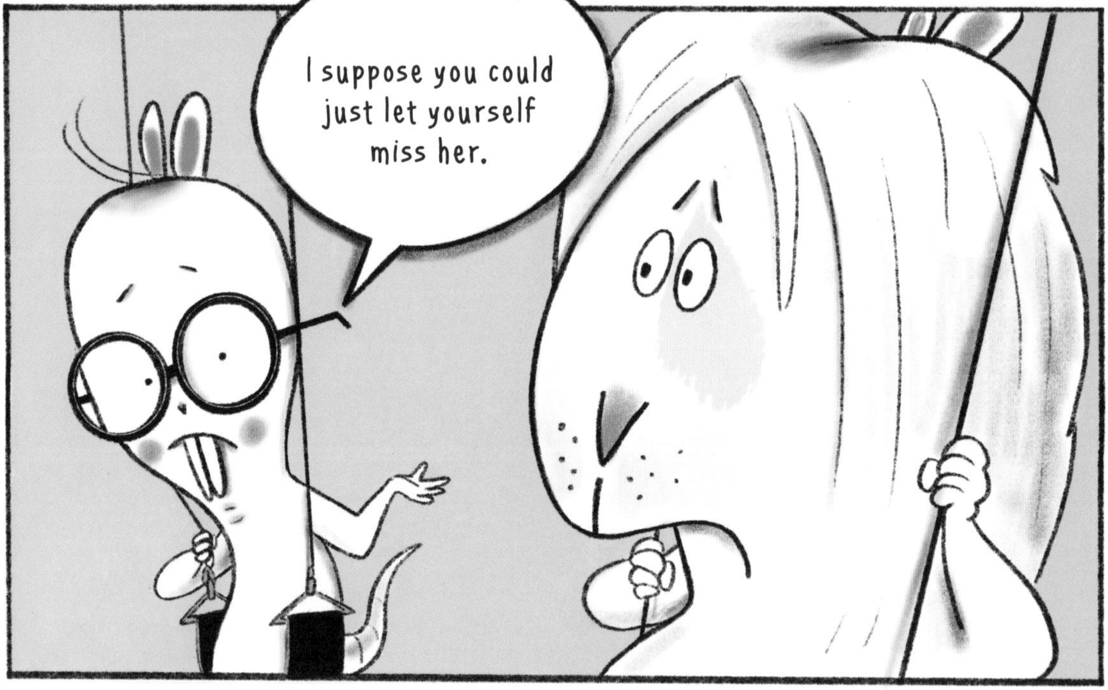
I suppose you could just let yourself miss her.

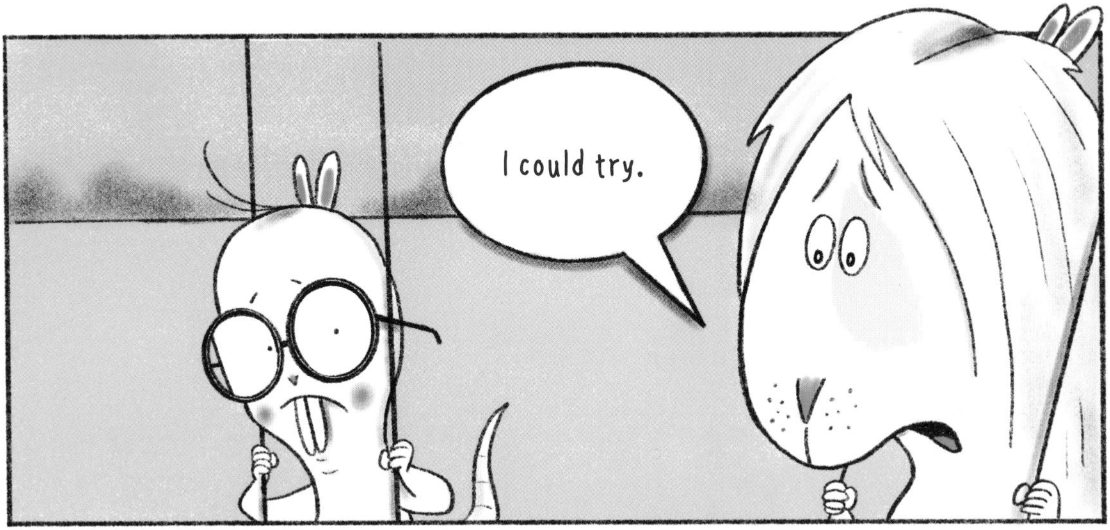
I could try.

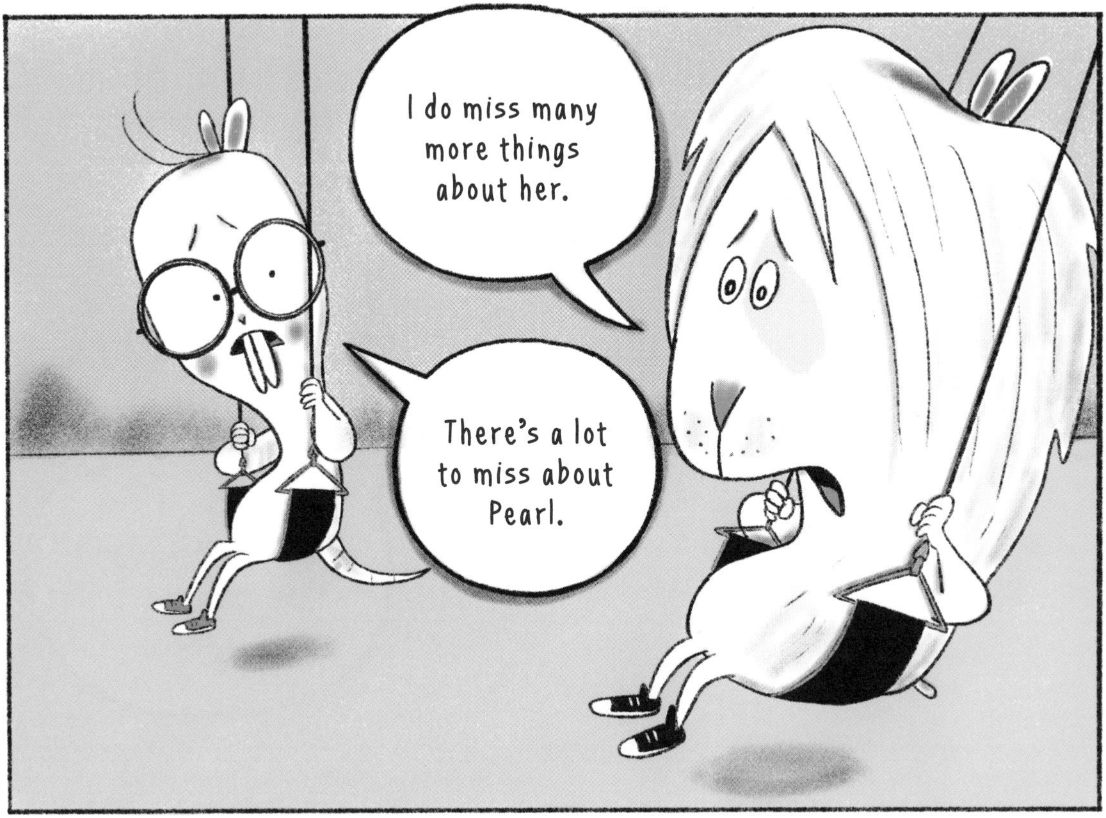
I do miss many more things about her.
There's a lot to miss about Pearl.

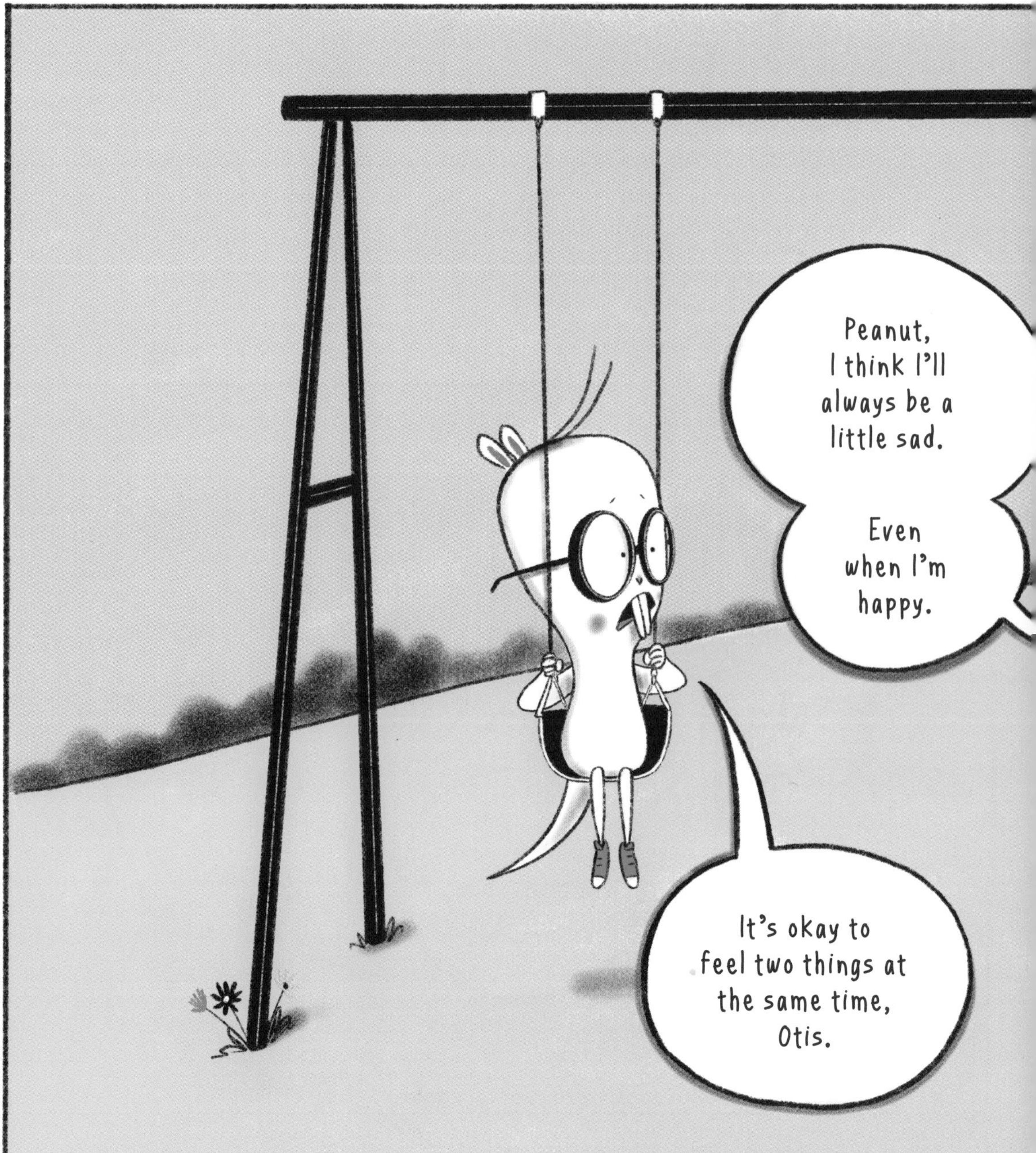
Peanut, I think I'll always be a little sad.
Even when I'm happy.
It's okay to feel two things at the same time, Otis.

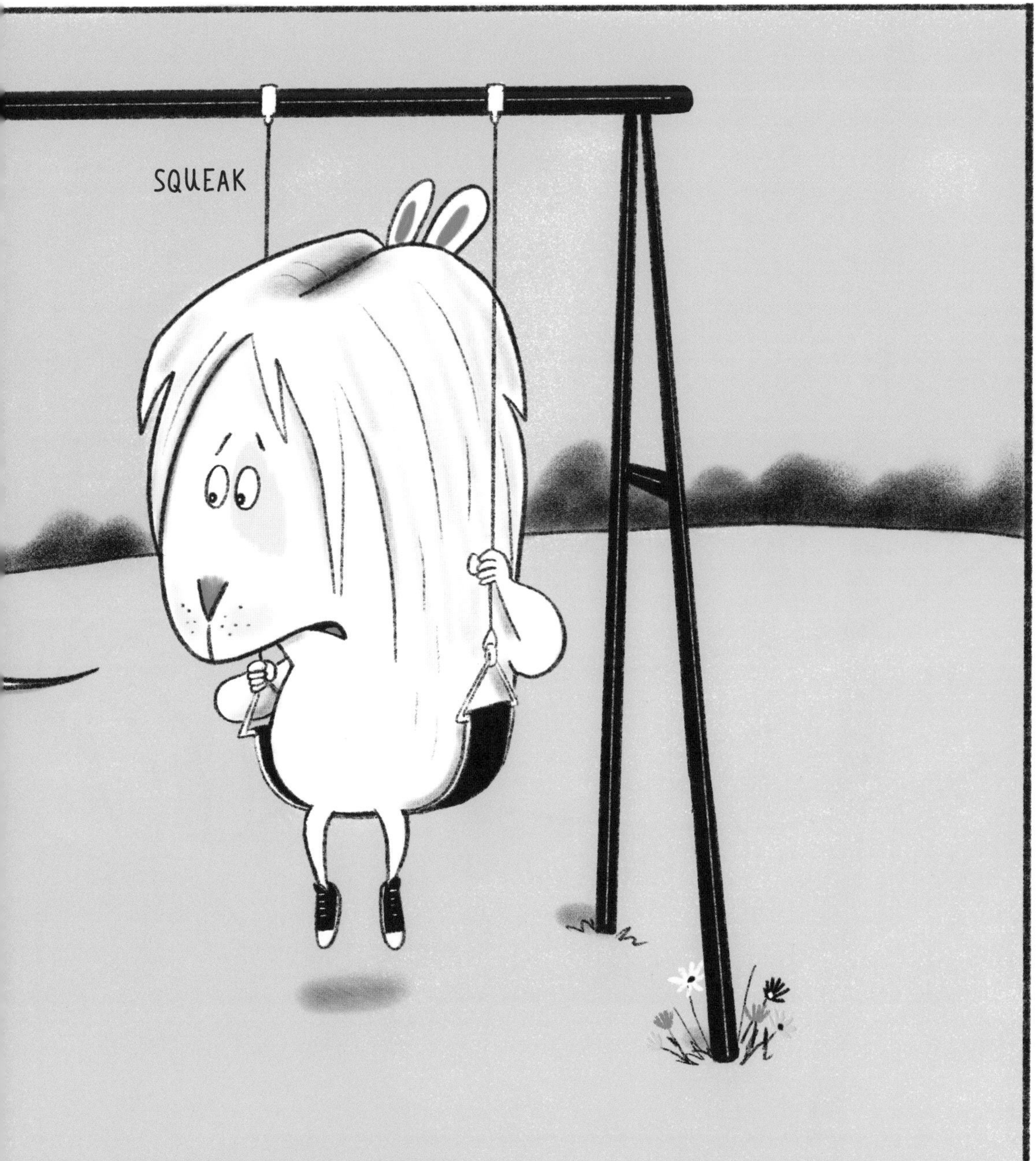
SQUEAK

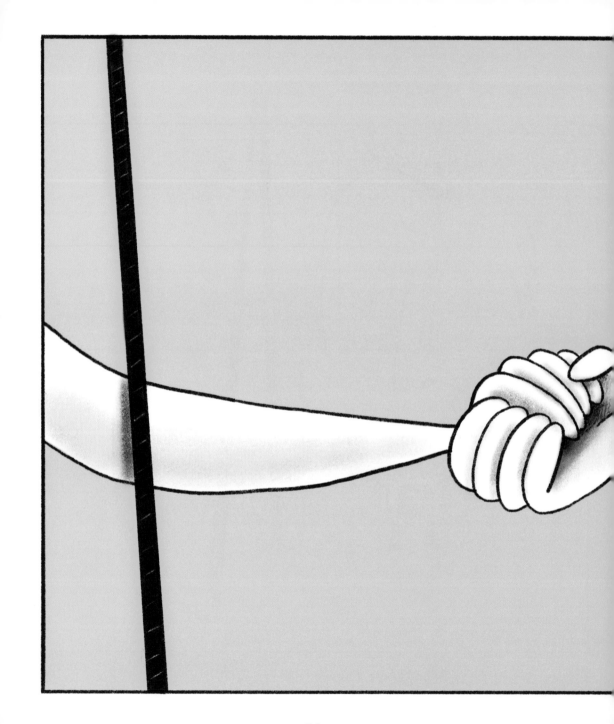

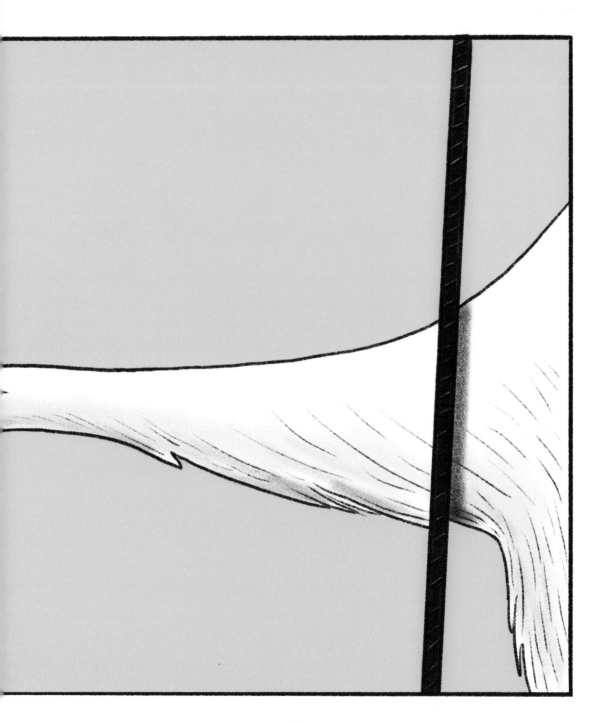

Then Otis and Peanut swung
back and forth together.

Only Otis swung a little bit
higher this time.

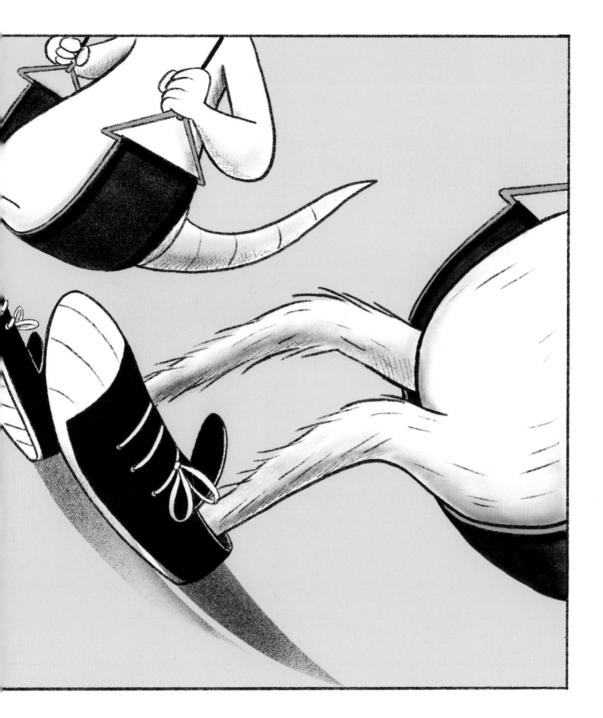

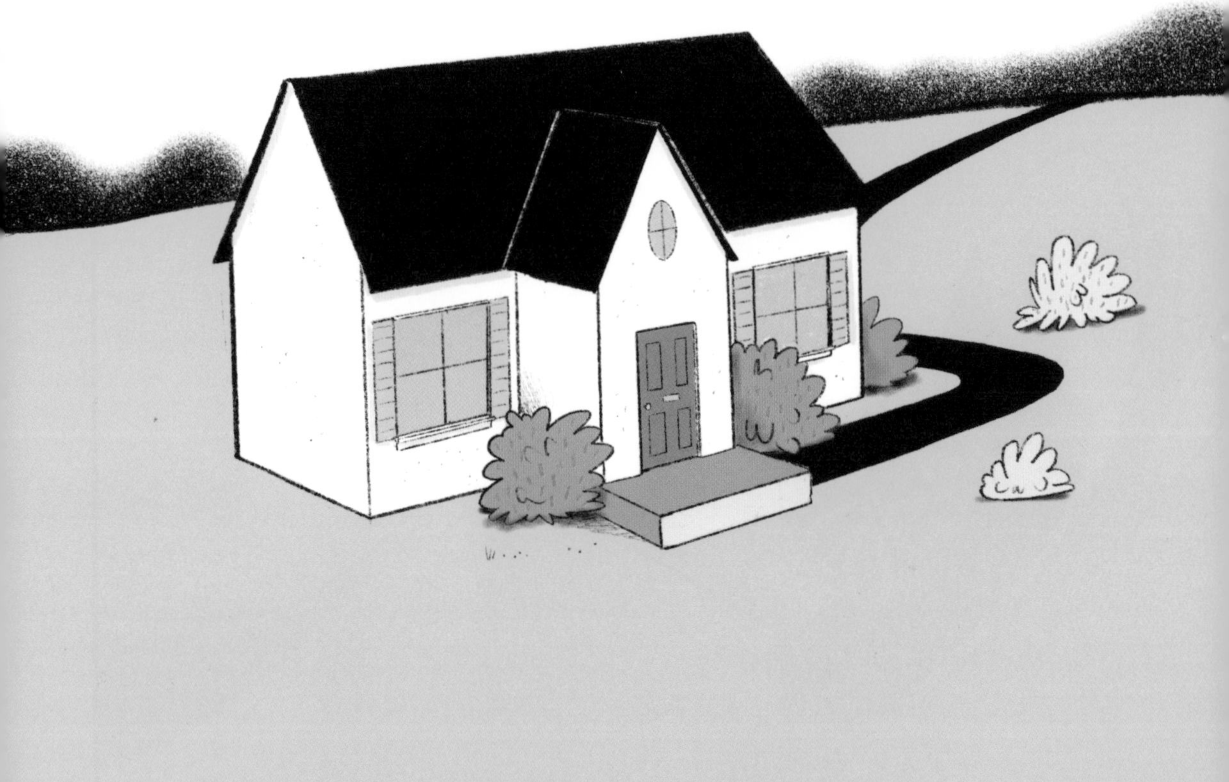

THE HOUSE

Peanut biked to Otis's new house for a visit.

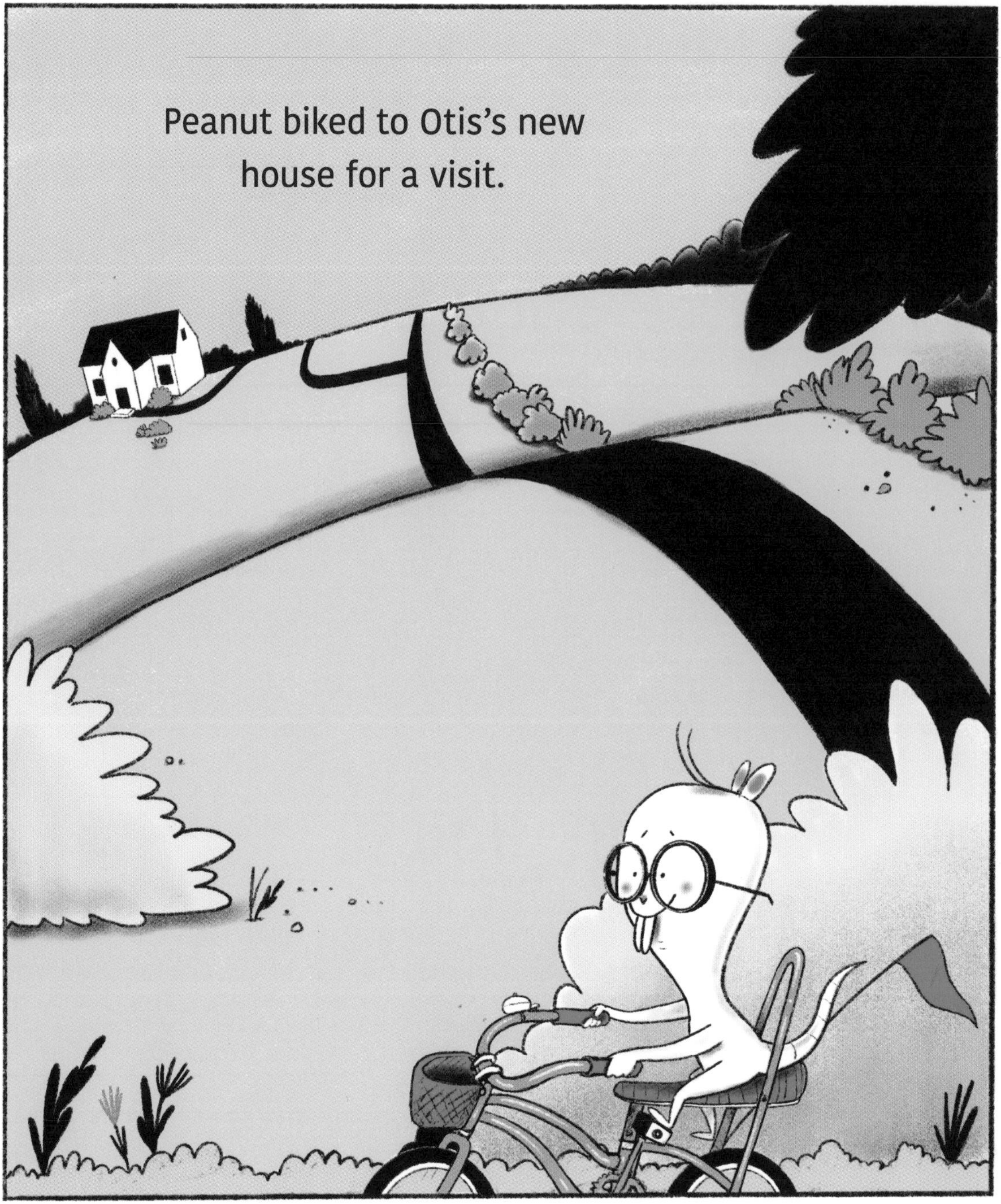

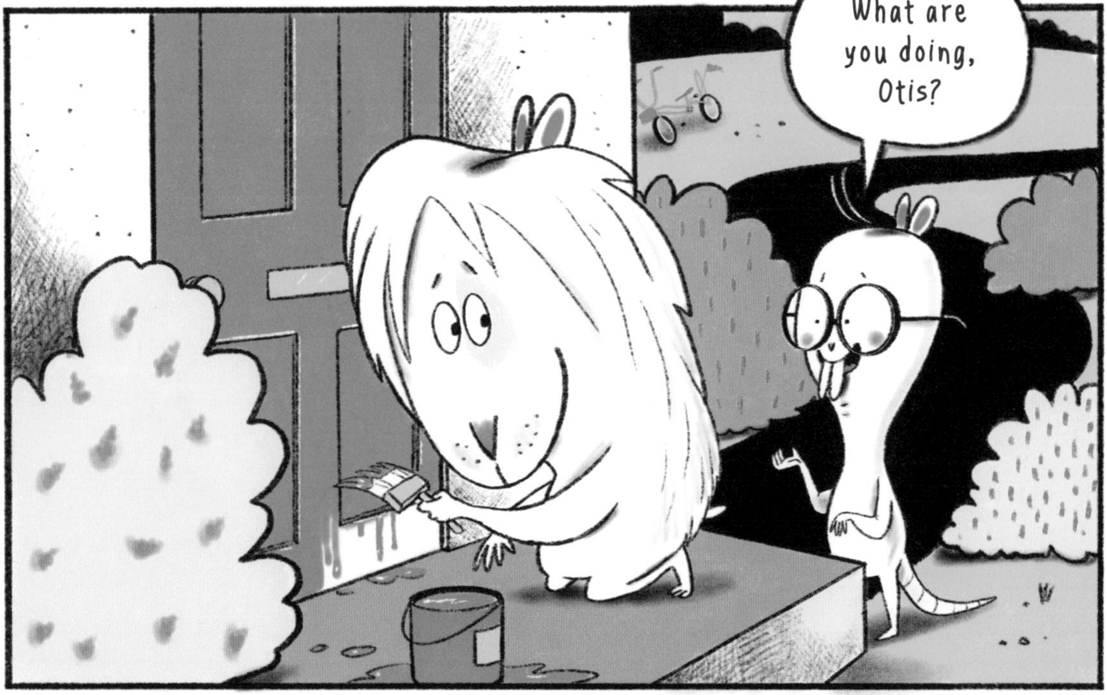
What are you doing, Otis?

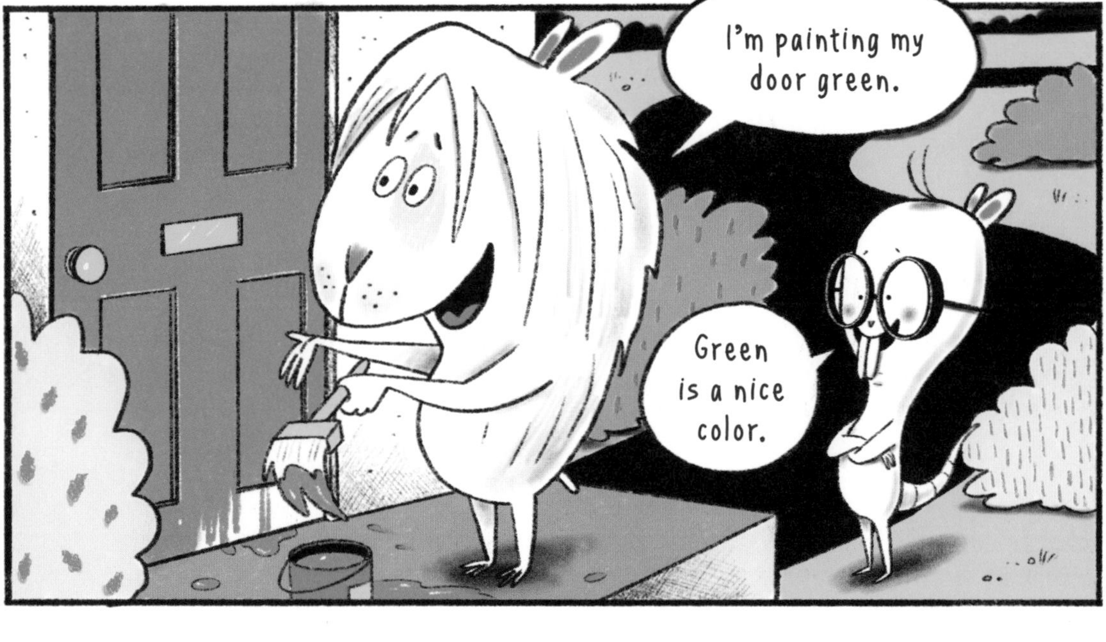
I'm painting my door green.
Green is a nice color.

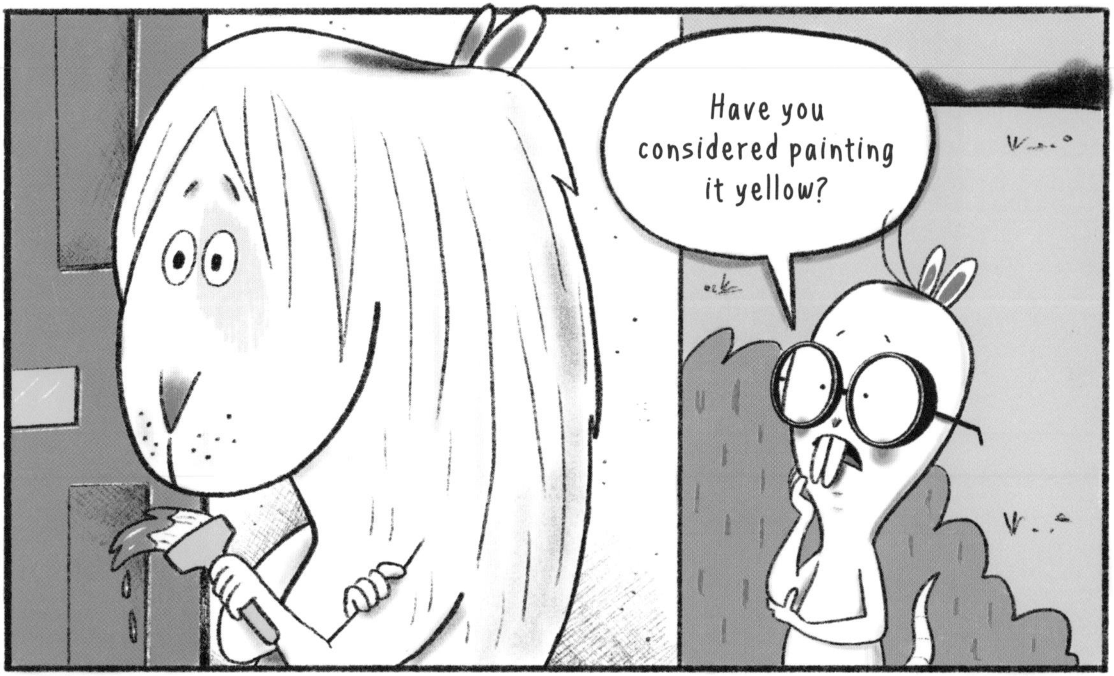
Have you considered painting it yellow?

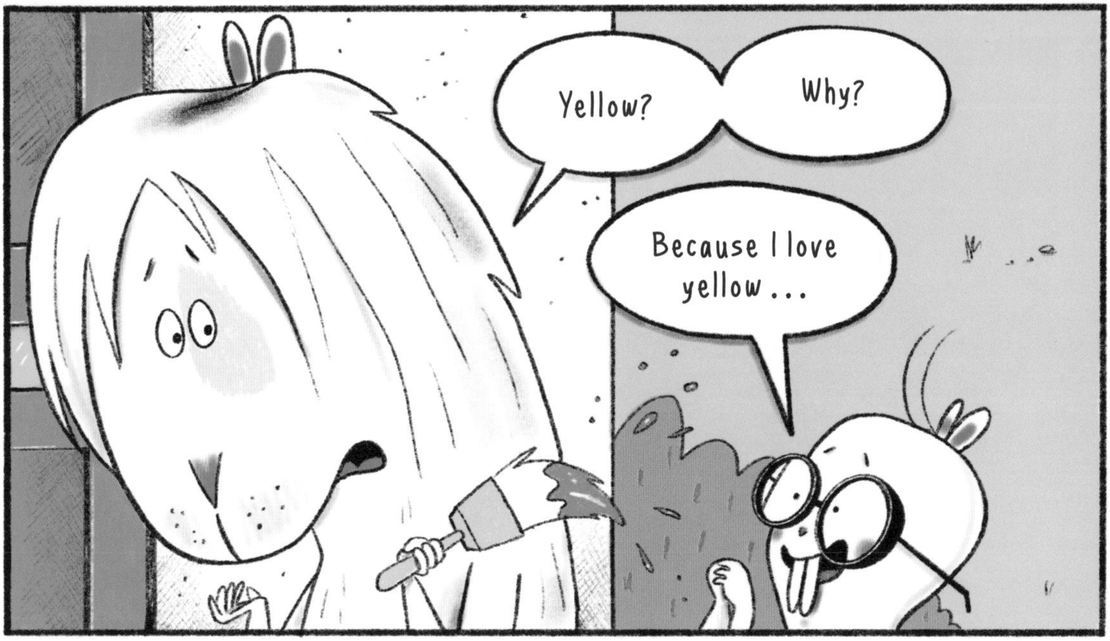
Yellow?
Why?
Because I love yellow . . .

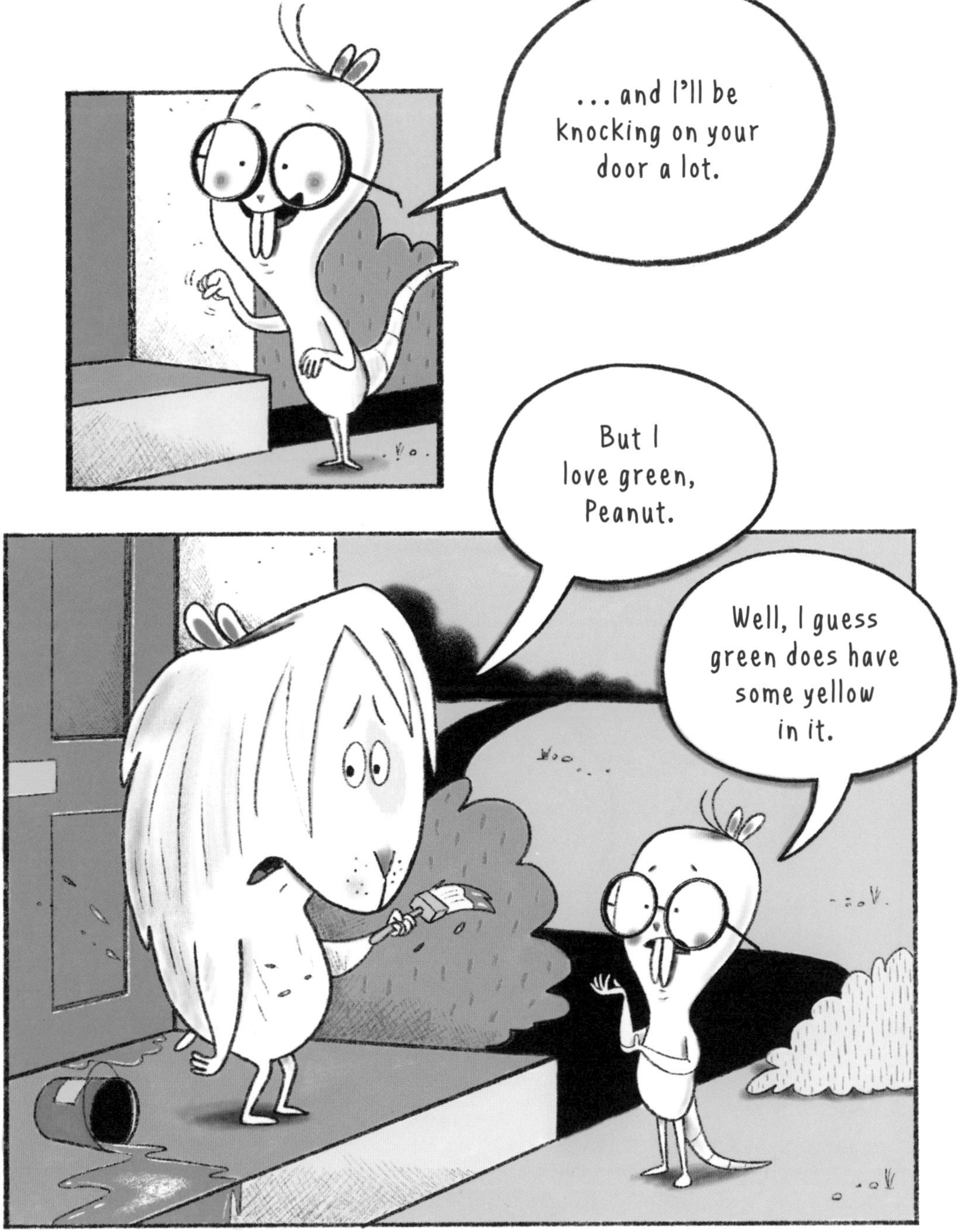

. . . and I'll be knocking on your door a lot.
But I love green, Peanut.
Well, I guess green does have some yellow in it.

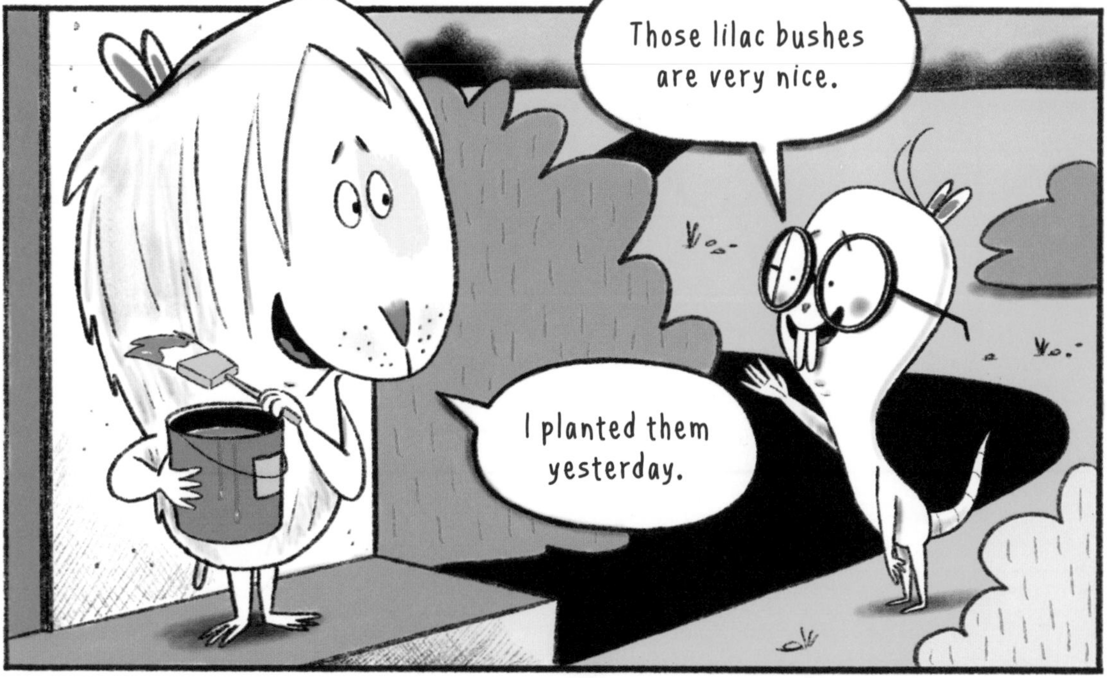
Those lilac bushes are very nice.
I planted them yesterday.

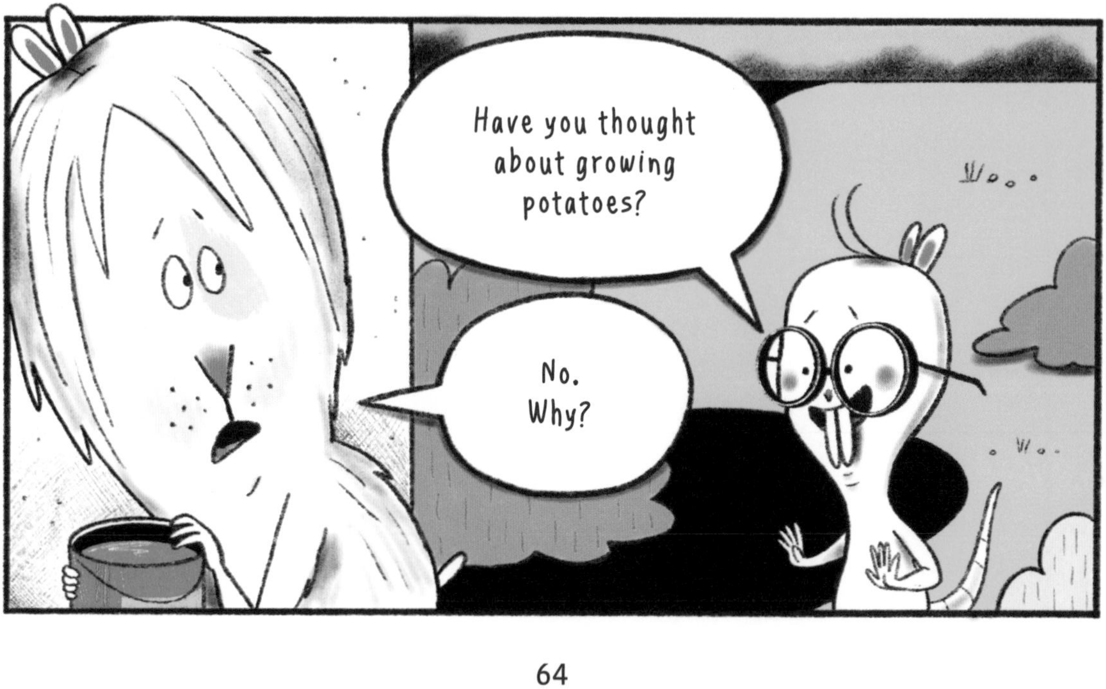
Have you thought about growing potatoes?
No. Why?

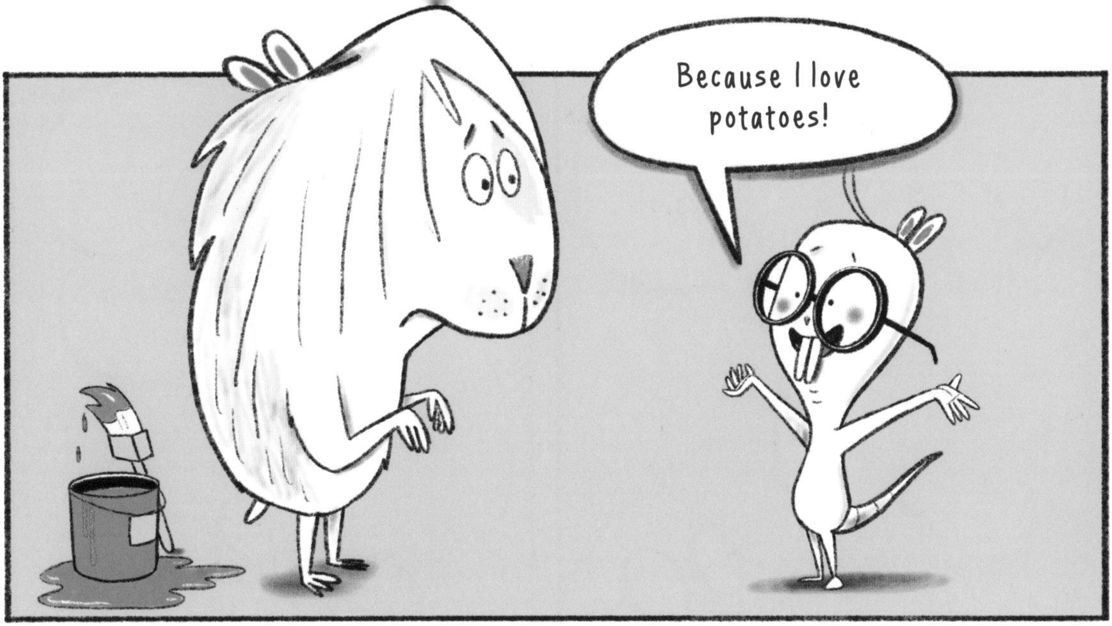
Because I love potatoes!

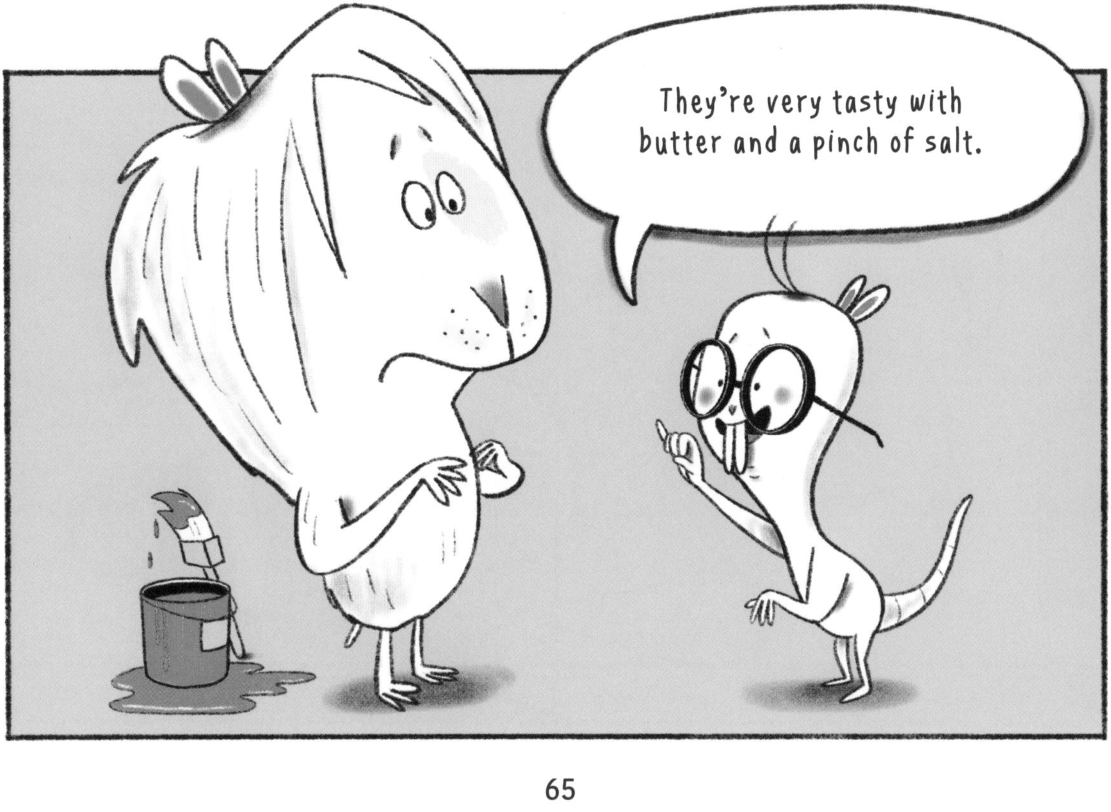
They're very tasty with butter and a pinch of salt.

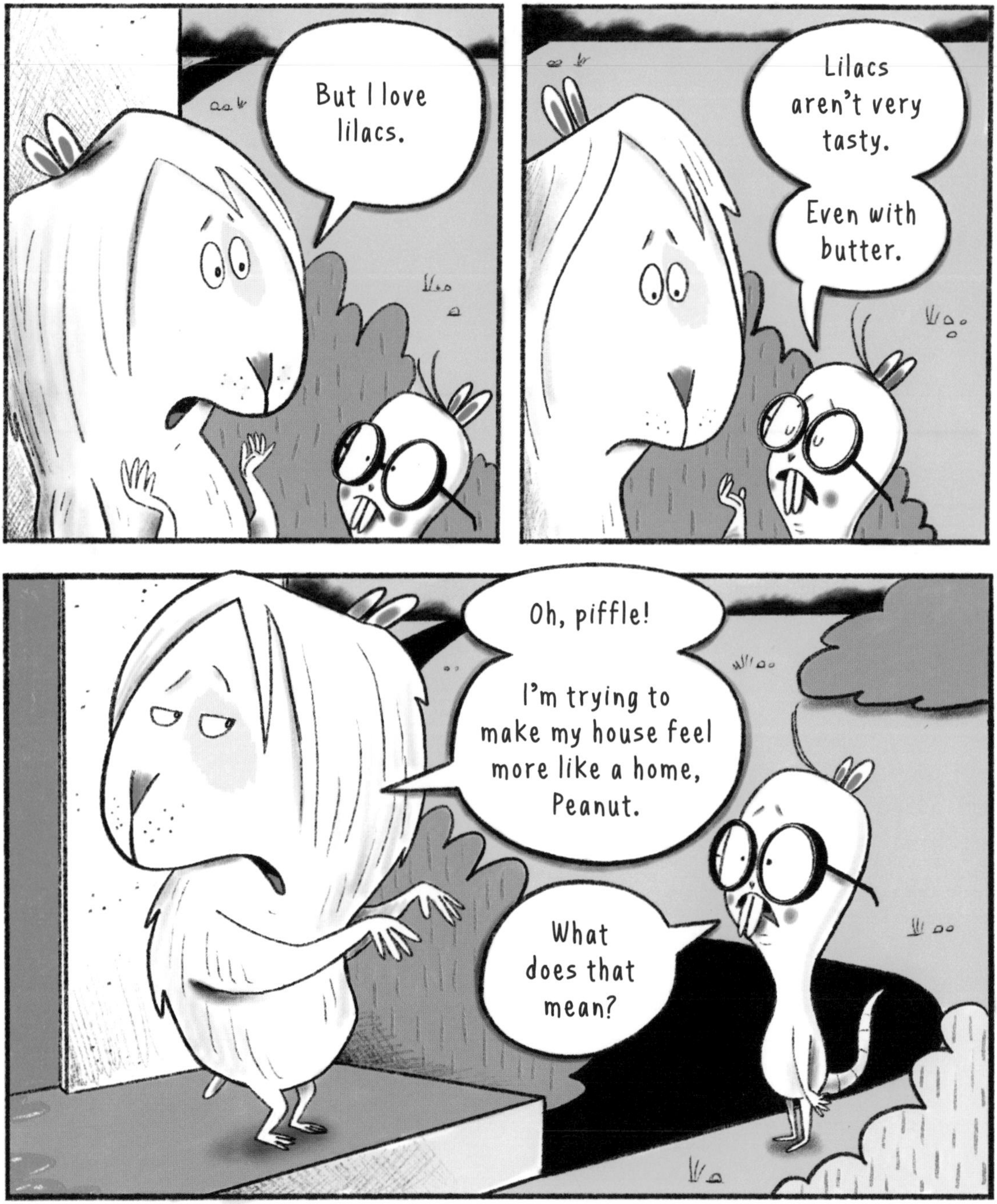
But I love lilacs.
Lilacs aren't very tasty.
Even with butter.
Oh, piffle!
I'm trying to make my house feel more like a home, Peanut.
What does that mean?

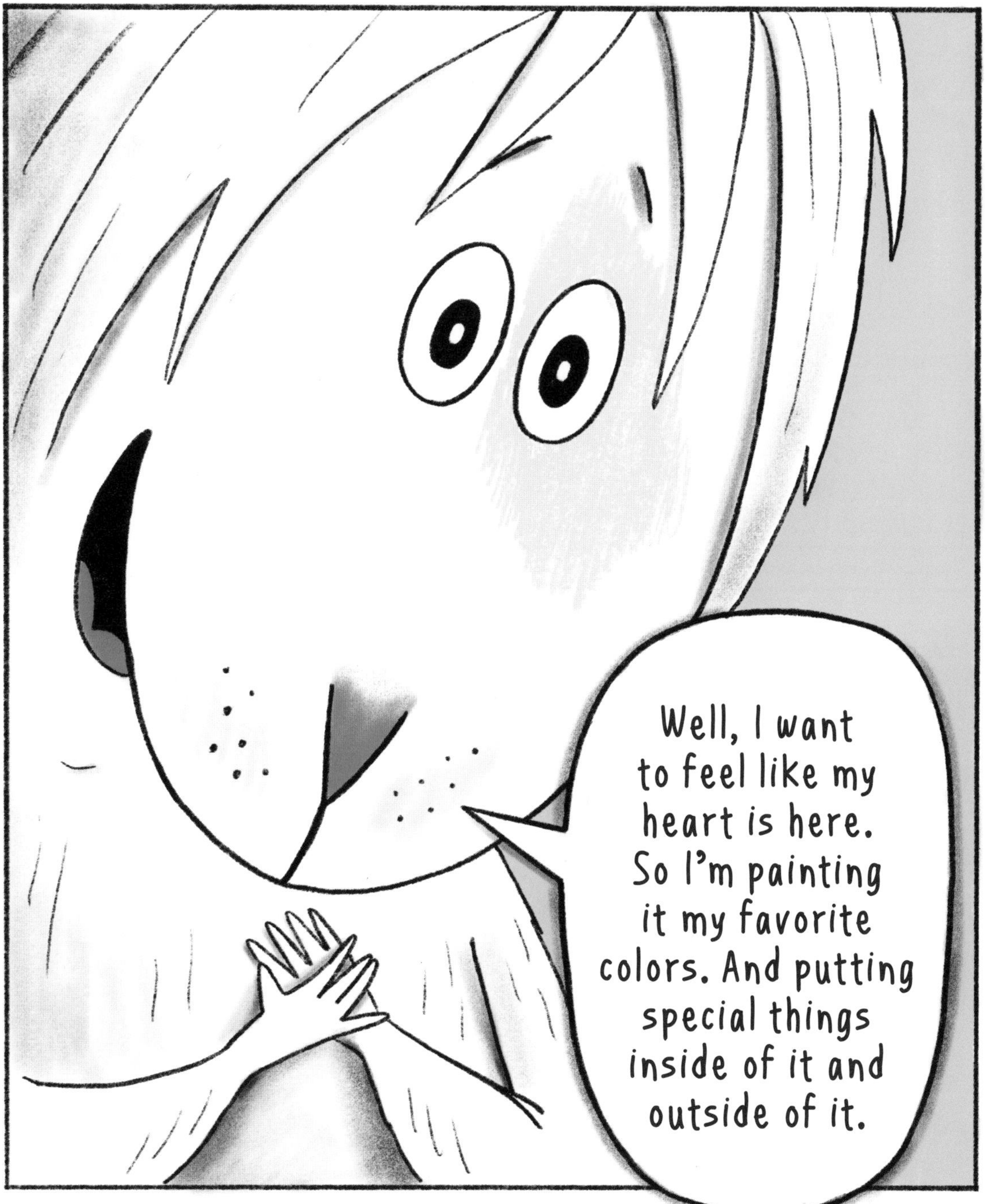
Well, I want to feel like my heart is here. So I'm painting it my favorite colors. And putting special things inside of it and outside of it.

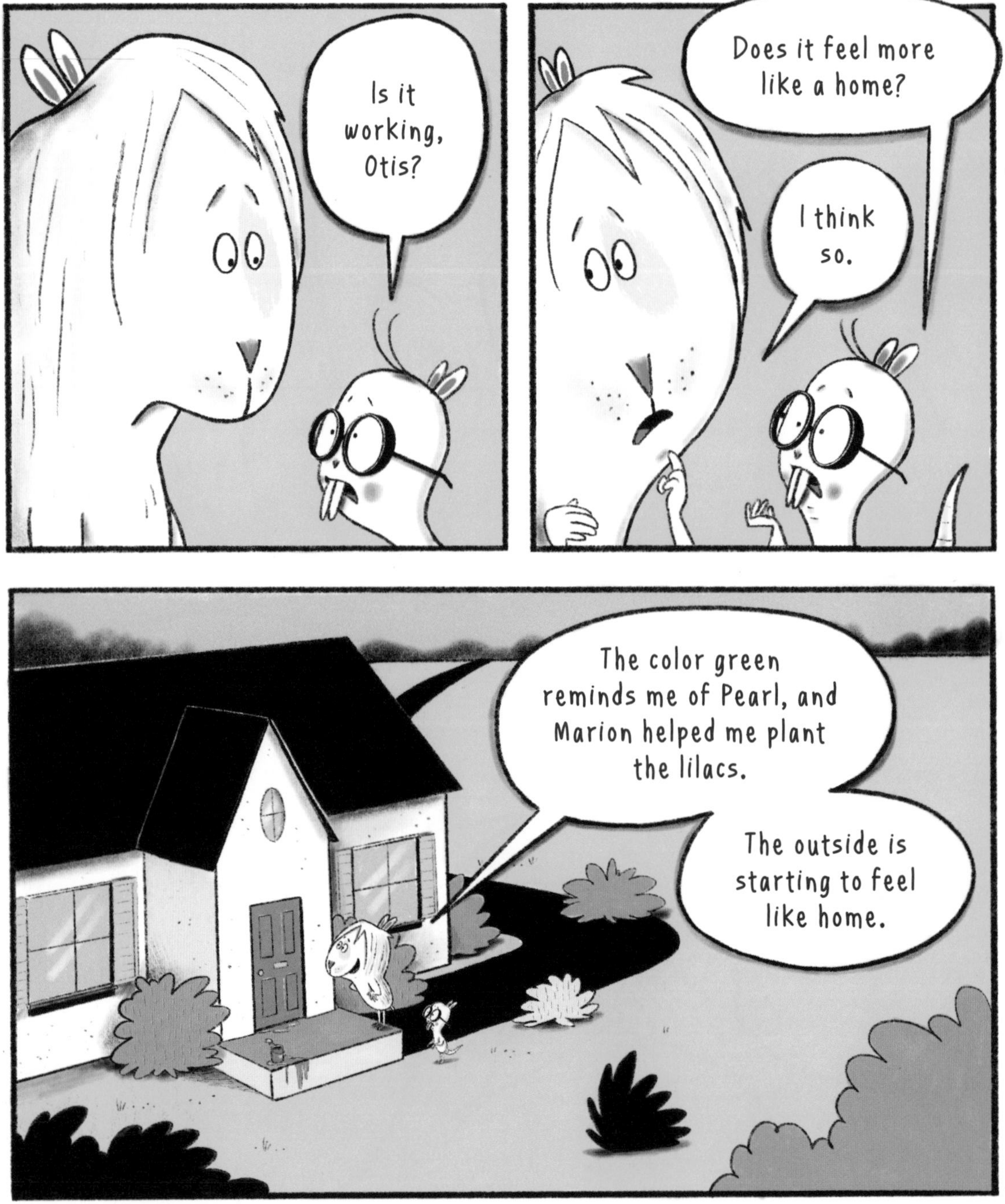
Is it working, Otis?
Does it feel more like a home?
I think so.
The color green reminds me of Pearl, and Marion helped me plant the lilacs.
The outside is starting to feel like home.

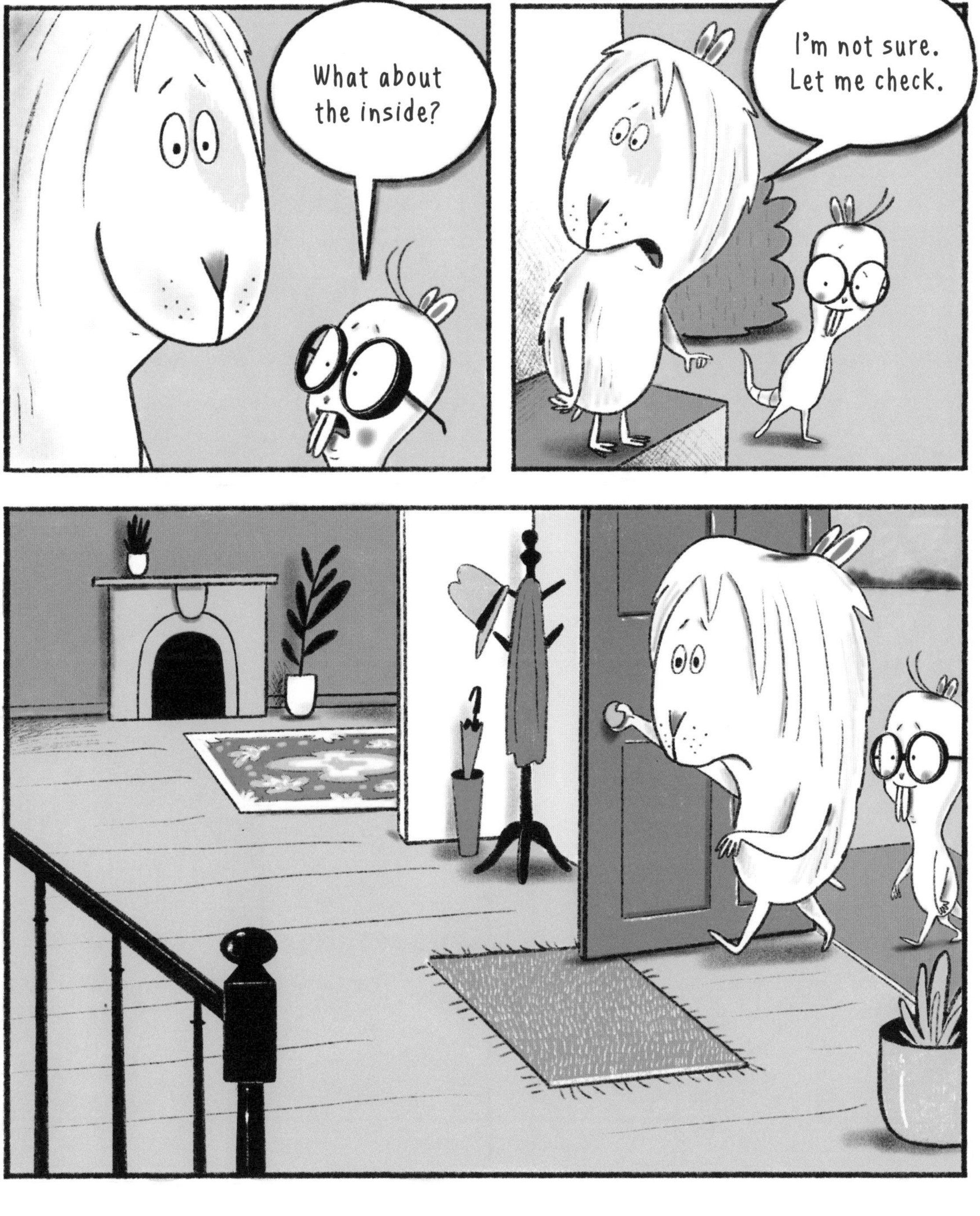
What about the inside?
I'm not sure. Let me check.

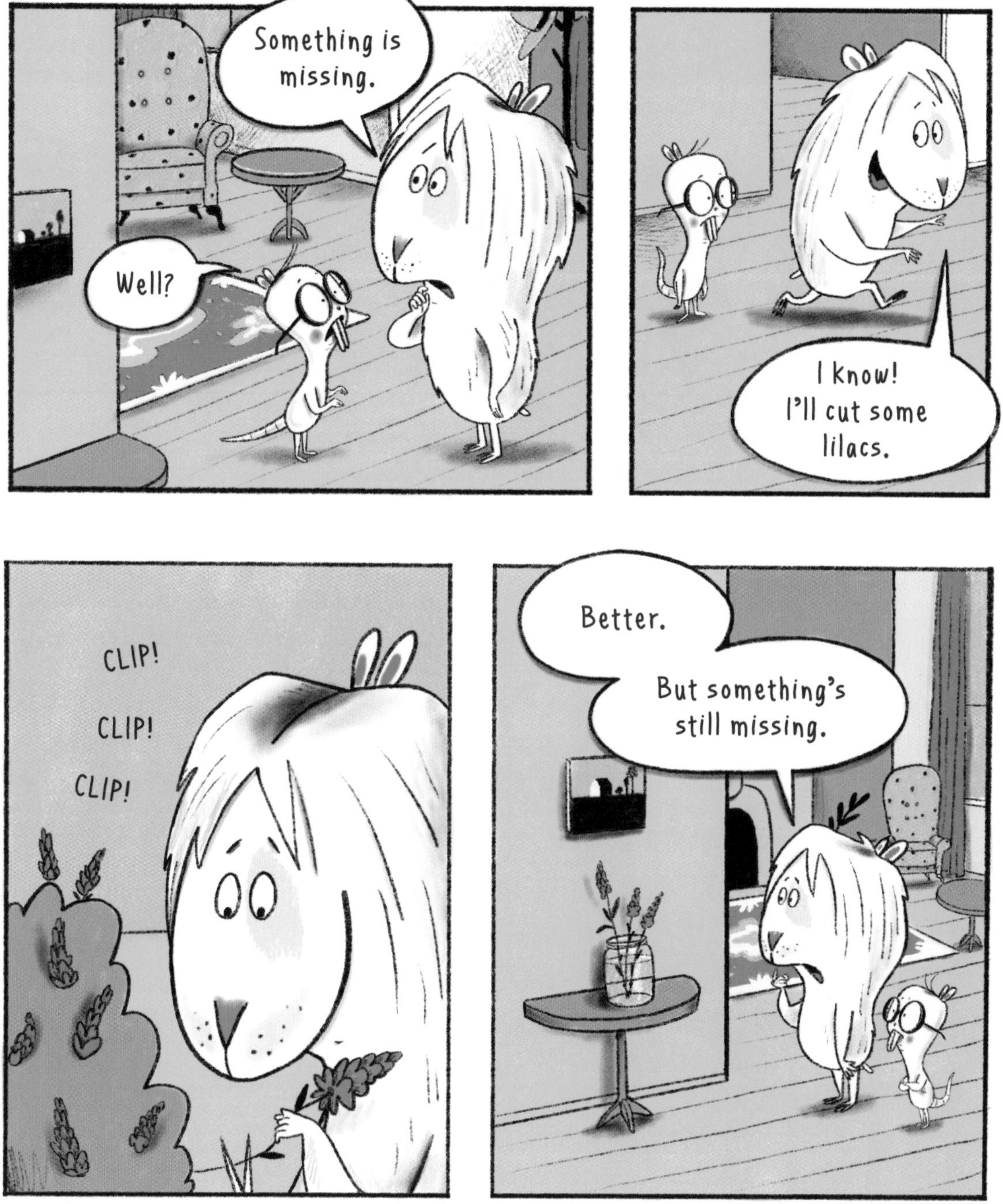
Something is missing.
Well?
I know! I'll cut some lilacs.
CLIP!
CLIP!
CLIP!
Better.
But something's still missing.

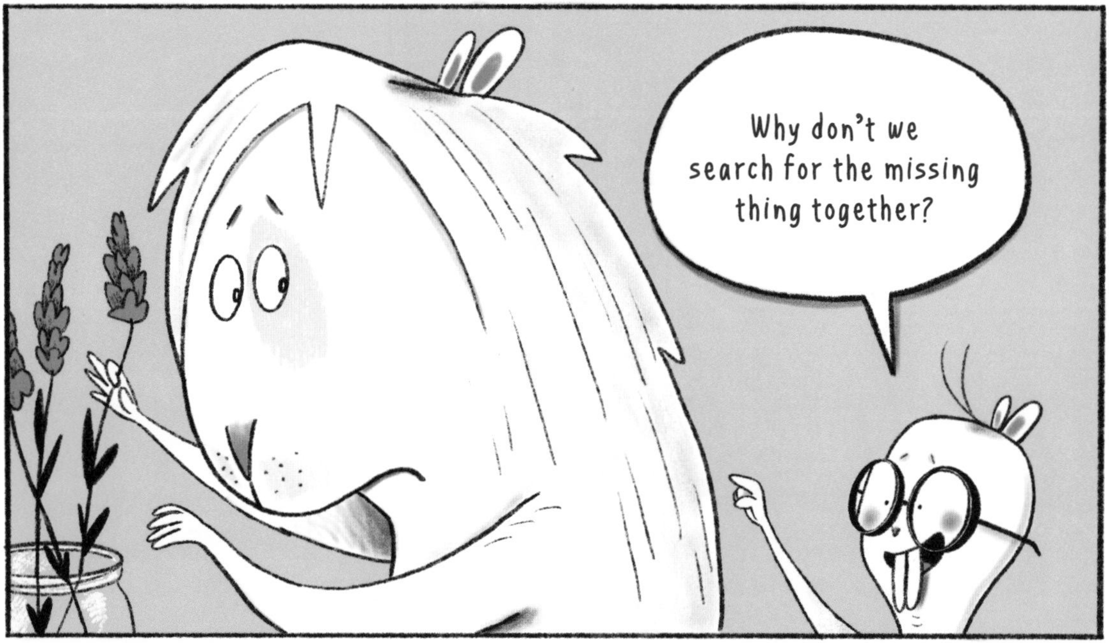
Why don't we search for the missing thing together?

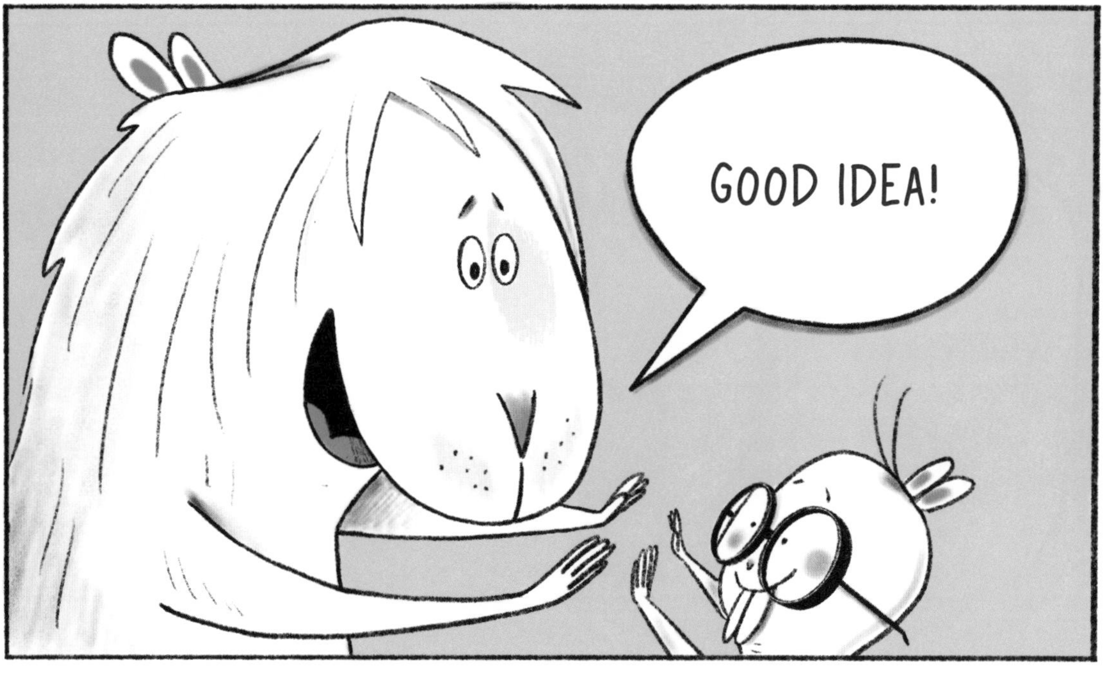
GOOD IDEA!

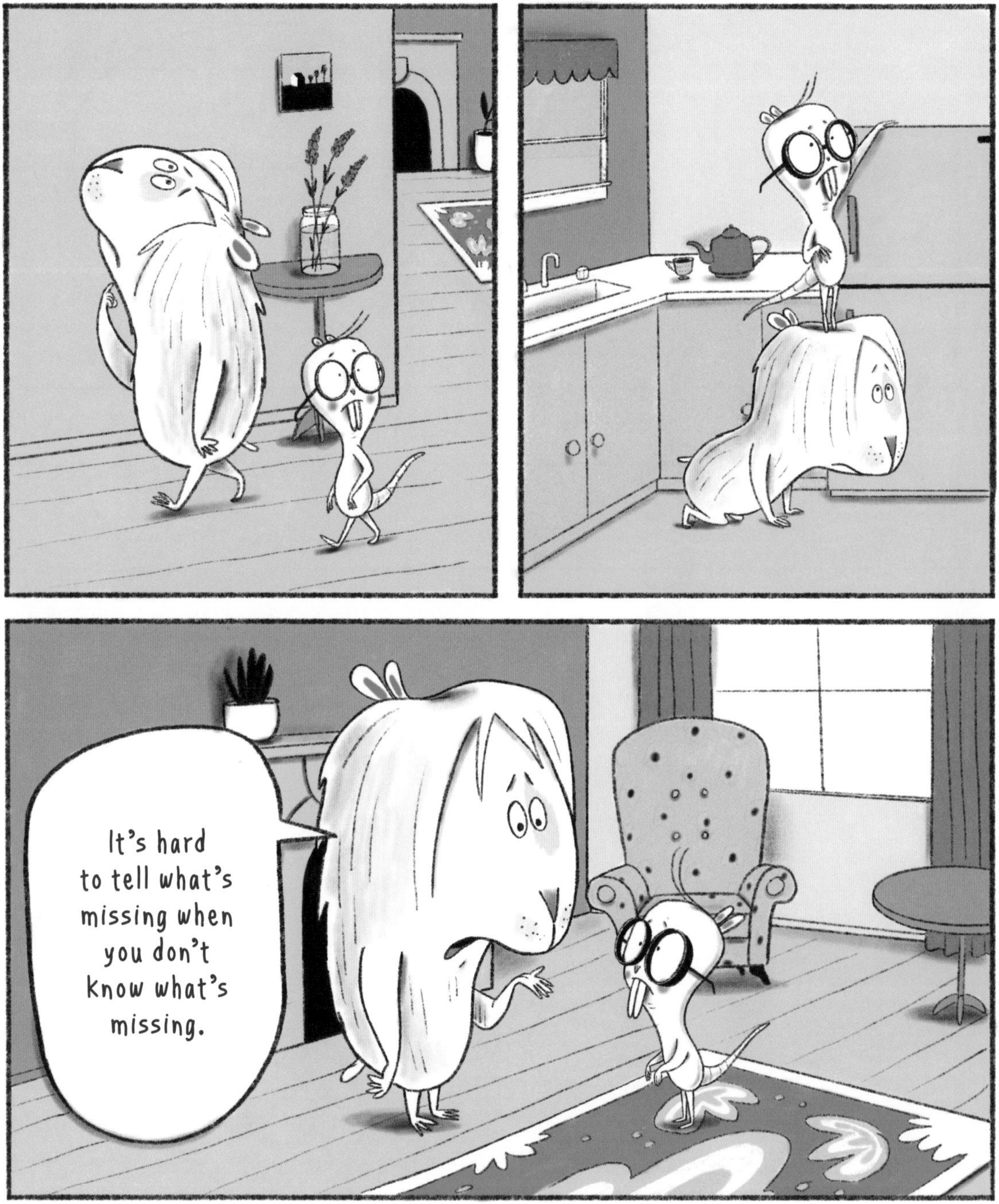
It's hard to tell what's missing when you don't know what's missing.

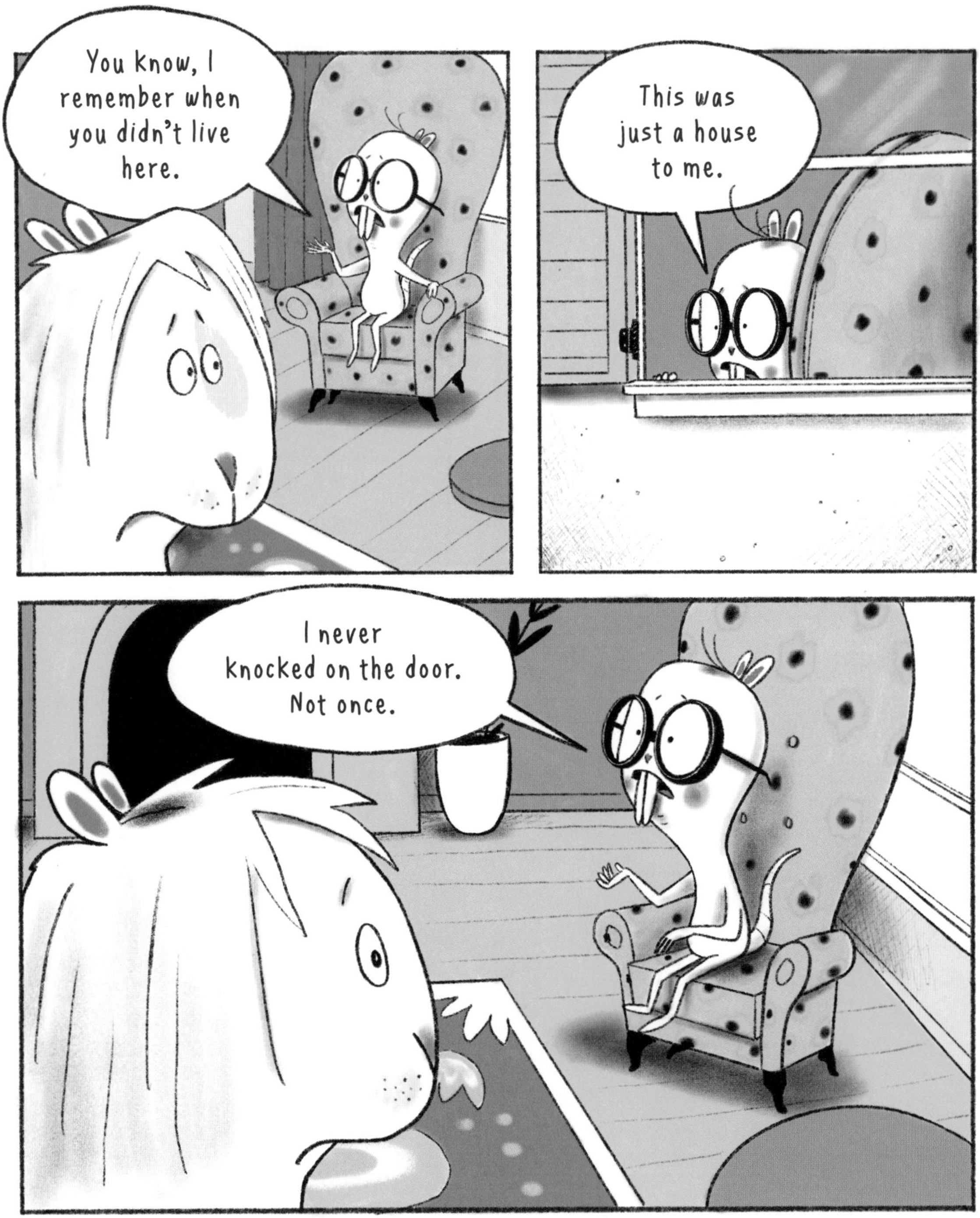
You know, I remember when you didn't live here.
This was just a house to me.
I never knocked on the door. Not once.

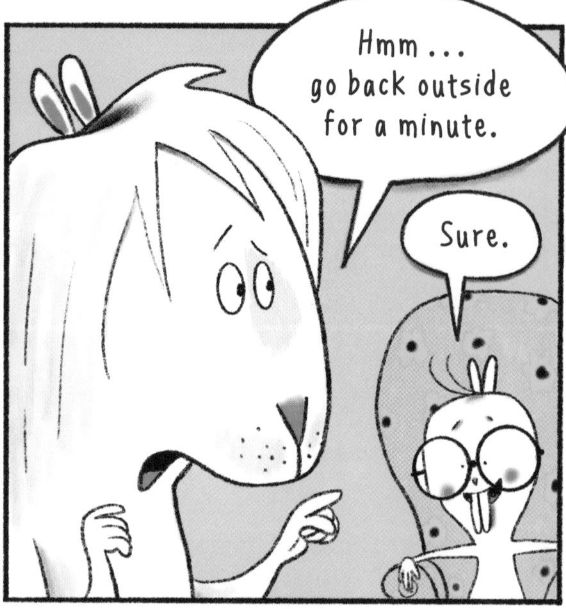
Hmm ...
go back outside
for a minute.
Sure.

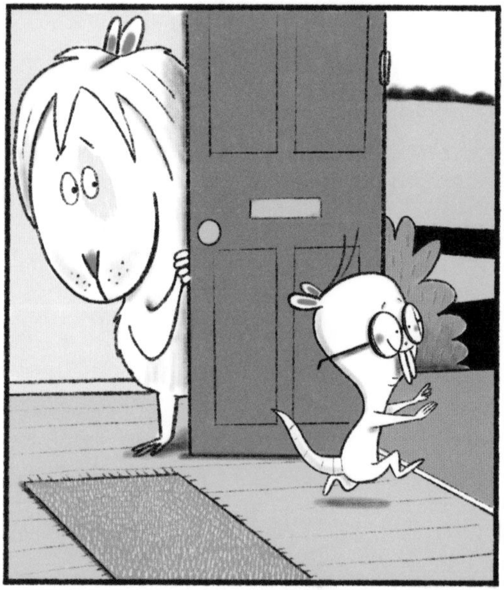

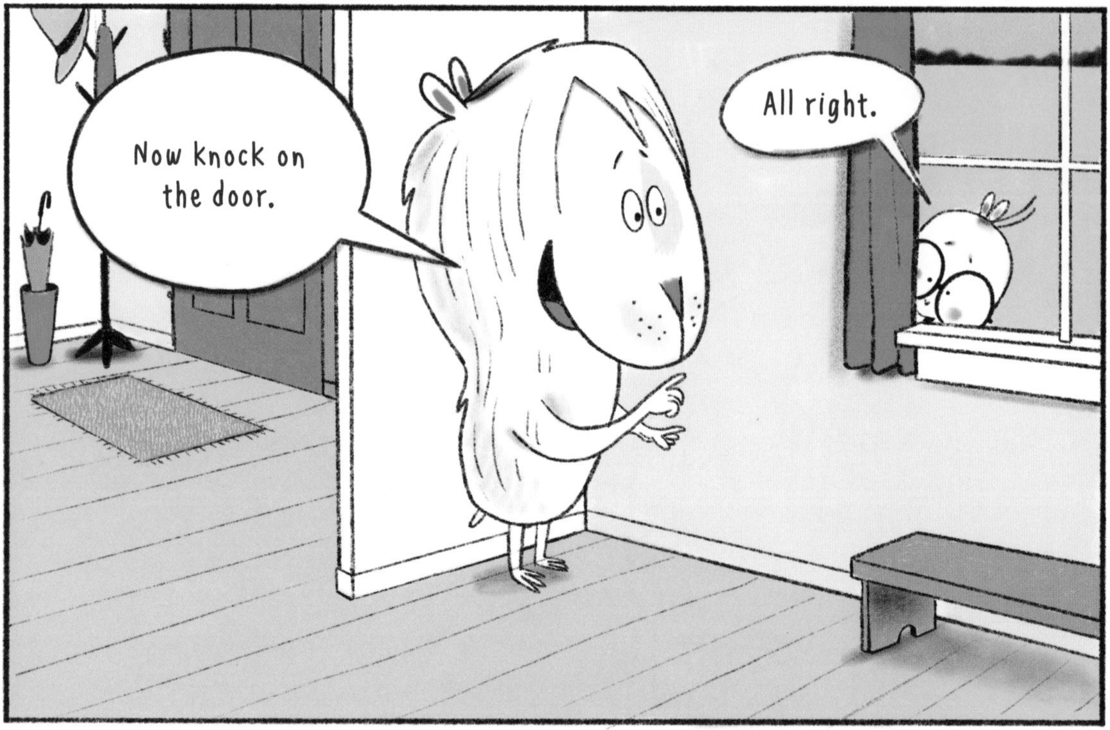
Now knock on
the door.
All right.

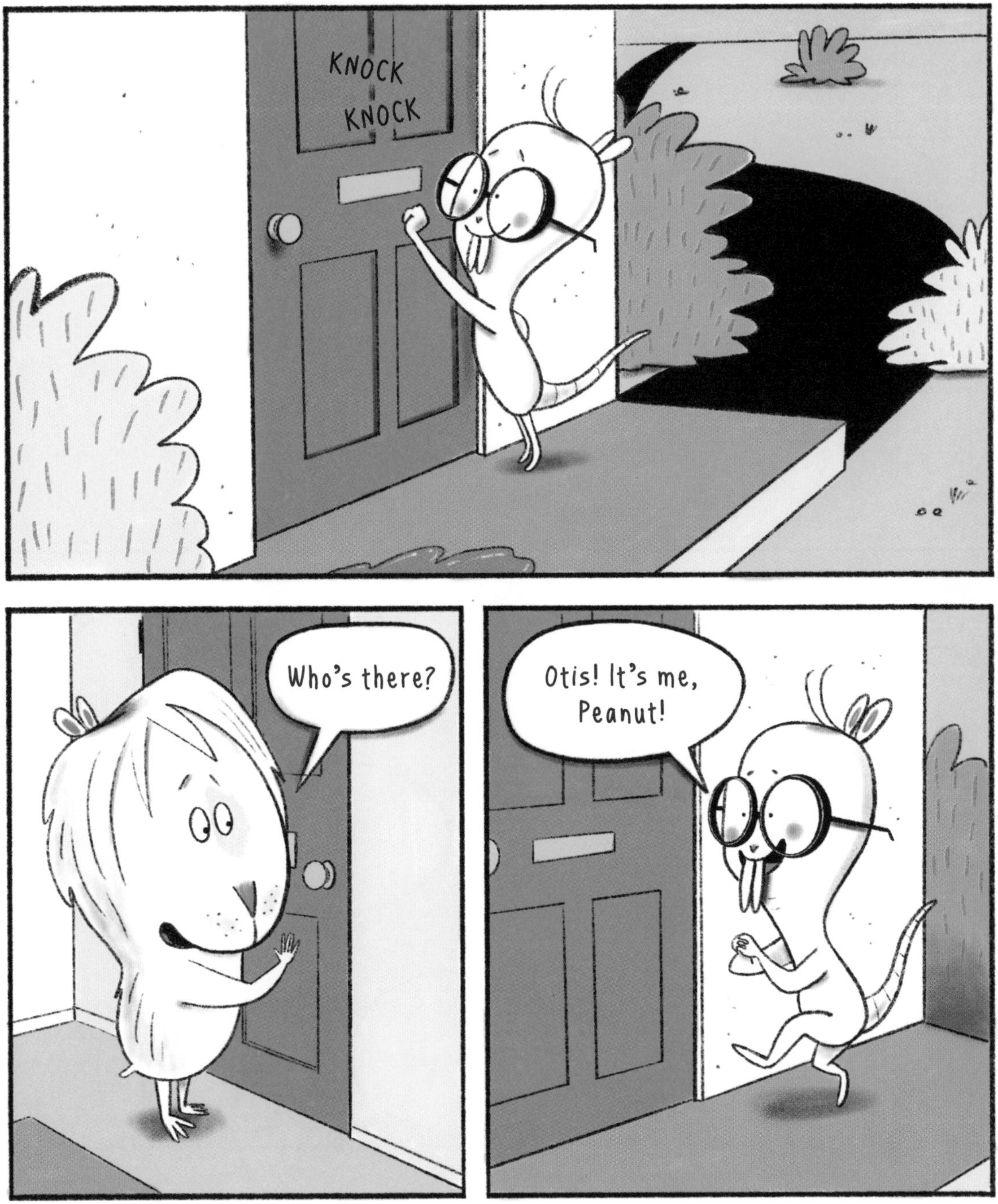
KNOCK
KNOCK
Who's there?
Otis! It's me, Peanut!

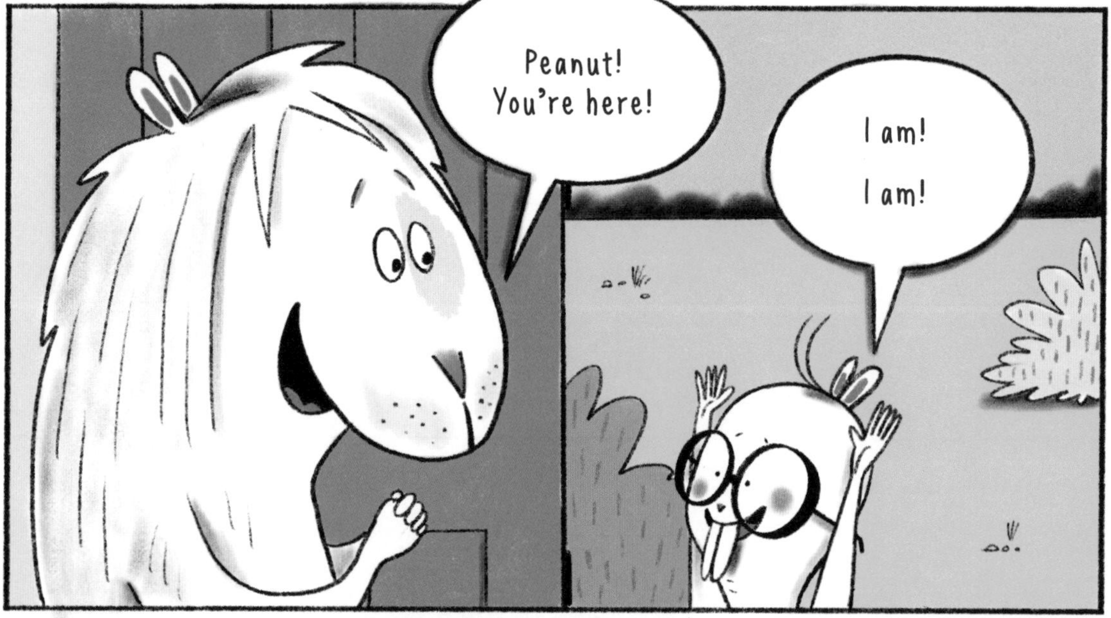
Peanut! You're here!
I am!
I am!

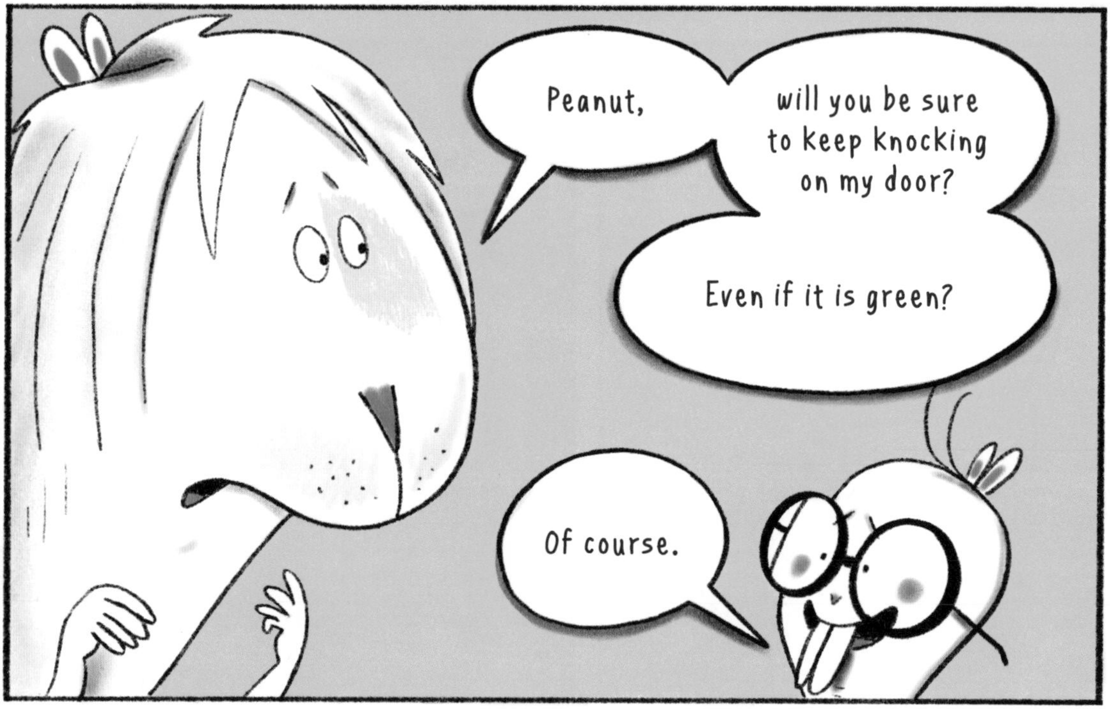
Peanut,
will you be sure to keep knocking on my door?
Even if it is green?
Of course.

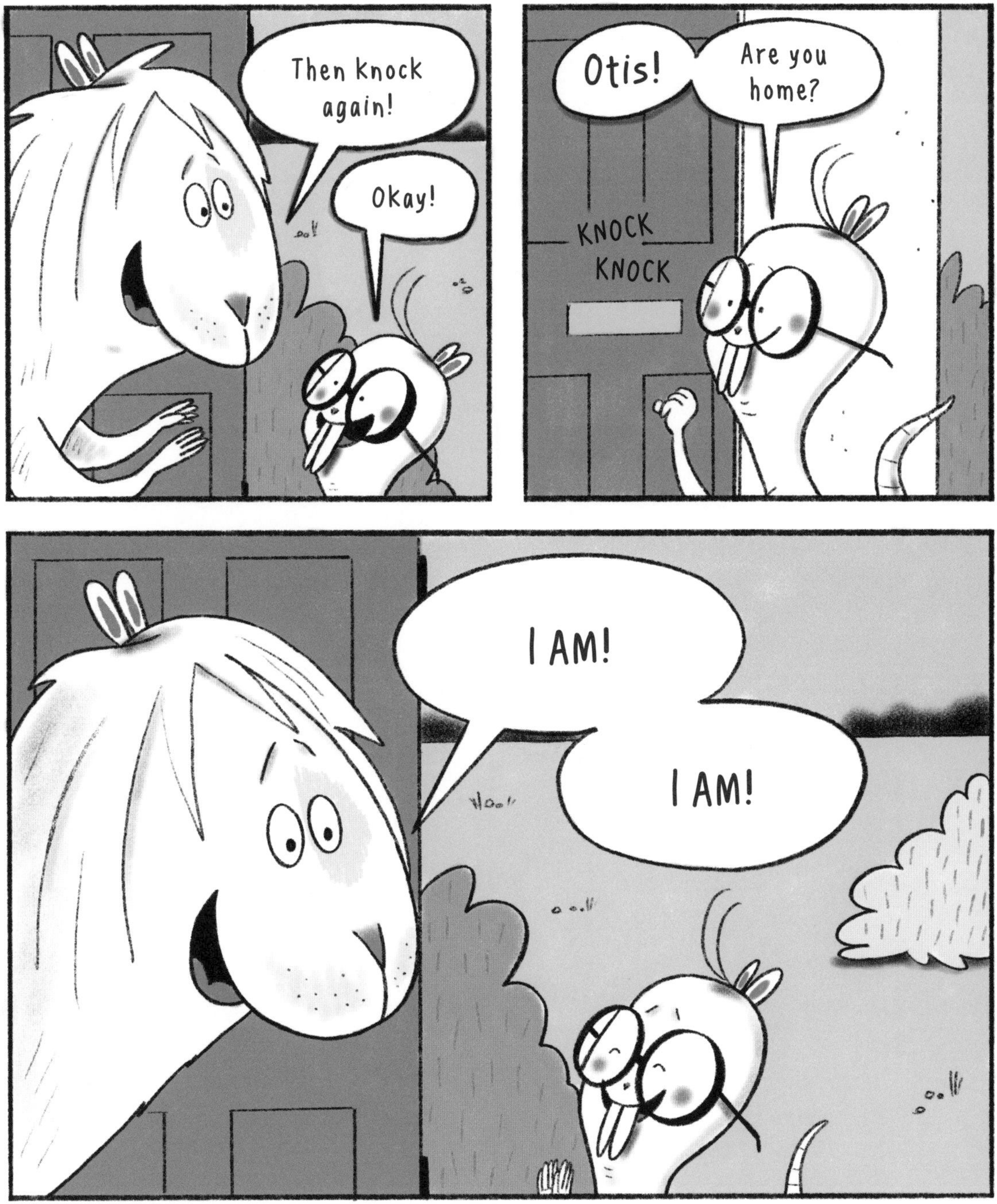
Then knock again!
Okay!
Otis!
Are you home?
KNOCK KNOCK
I AM!
I AM!

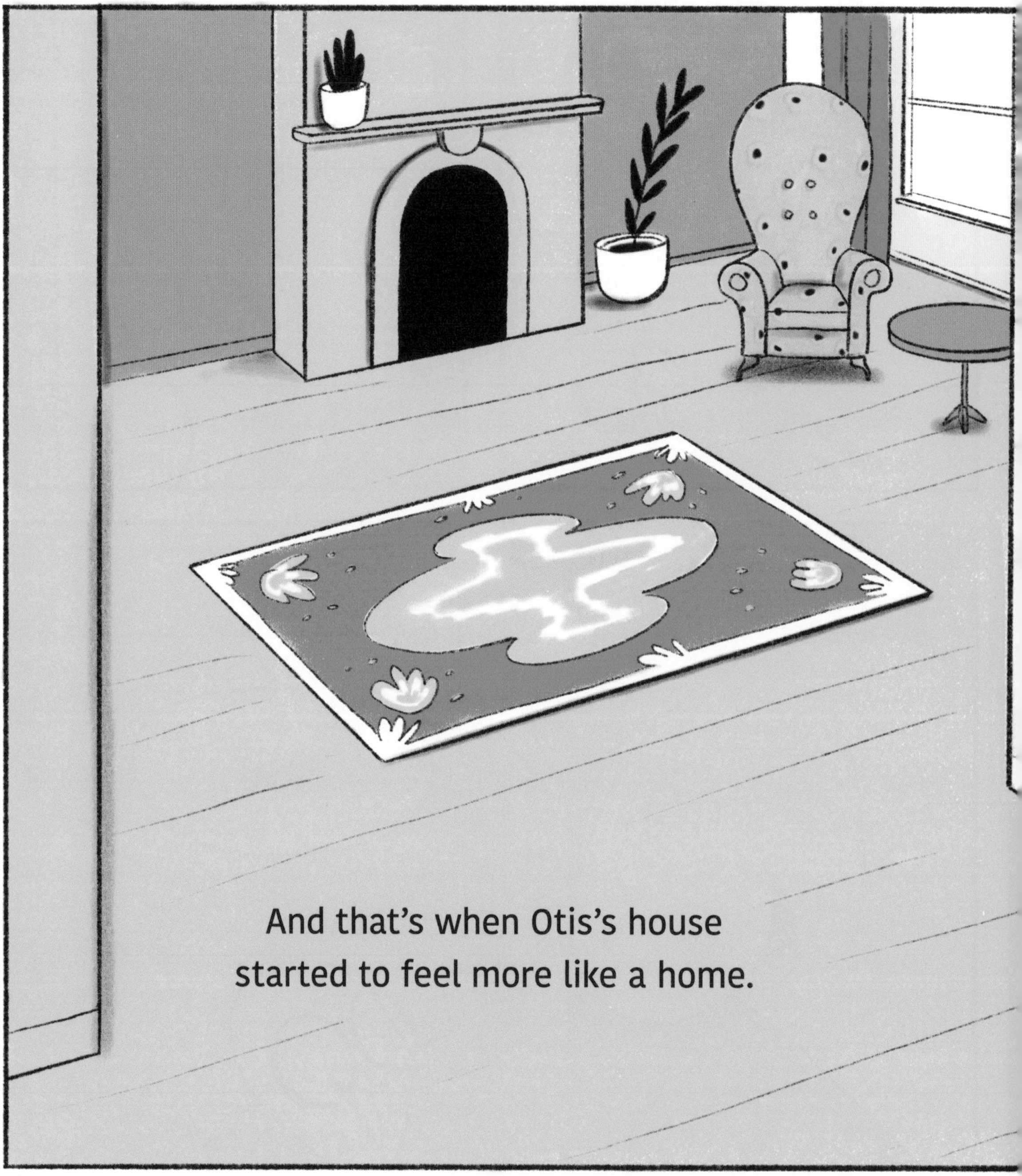
And that's when Otis's house
started to feel more like a home.

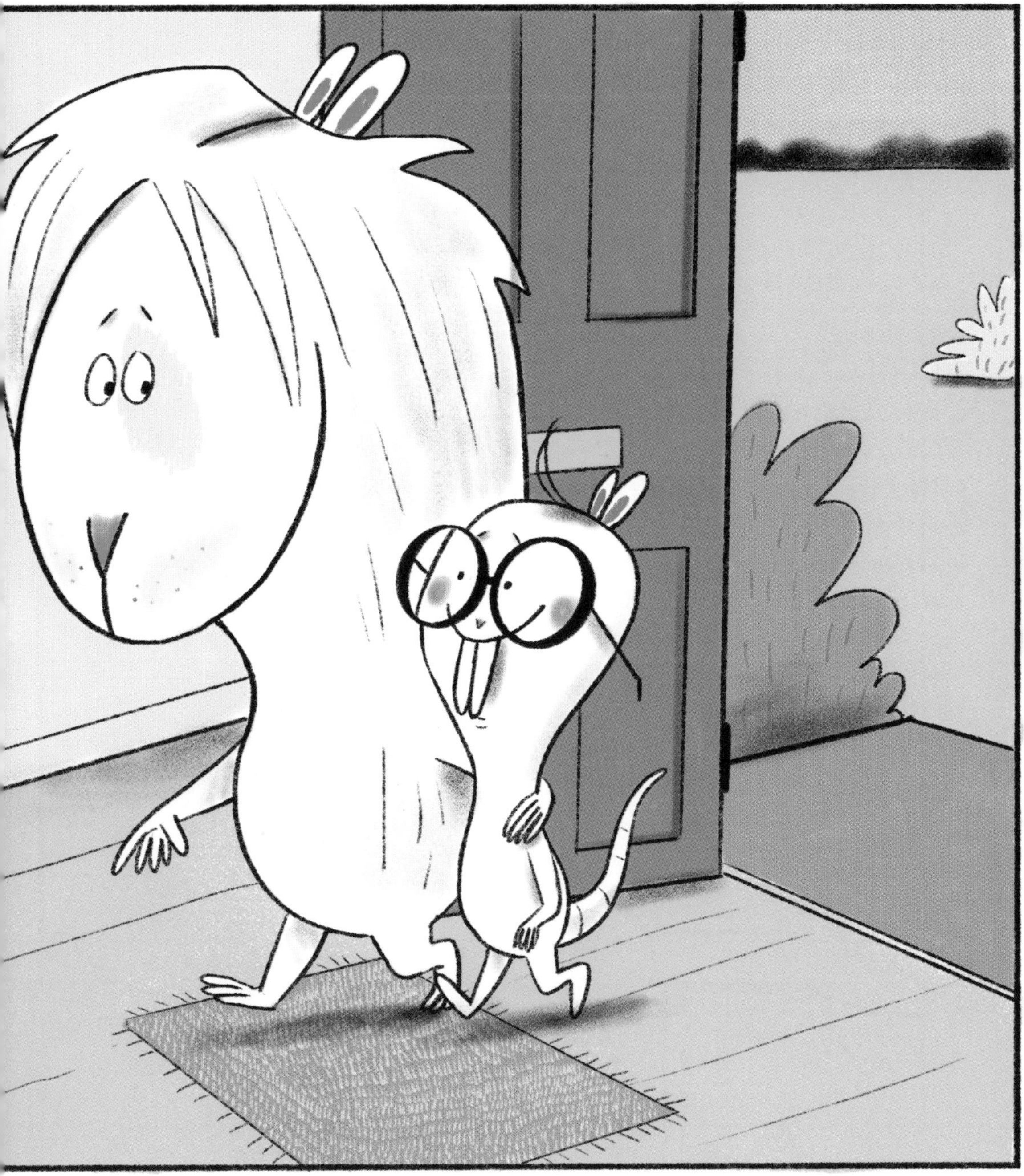

Peanut's Perfect Baked Potatoes for Two

Ingredients:

- 2 large potatoes
- 1 tbsp. (15 mL) olive oil
- salt and butter to taste

Directions:

1. Ask your adult to preheat the oven to 350°F (180°C).
2. Give your potatoes a bath—wash, scrub, and dry them.
3. Using a fork, carefully poke several deep holes into the potatoes.
4. Place the potatoes in a bowl and coat with olive oil.
5. Sprinkle with two generous pinches of salt.
6. Ask your adult to place the potatoes on the middle rack of the preheated oven.
7. After about forty-five minutes, ask your adult to wear an oven mitt and check on the potatoes. Gently squeeze the potatoes. (They'll be hot!) If the insides are soft, they're done. If they're still firm, continue cooking them for about ten minutes.
8. Once the potatoes are cooked through, carefully split them open lengthwise with a knife and fluff the insides with a fork.
9. Butter and salt to taste!

I got you a present, Otis!
Did you already take a bite of it?
I had to make sure it was tasty.
And it is!

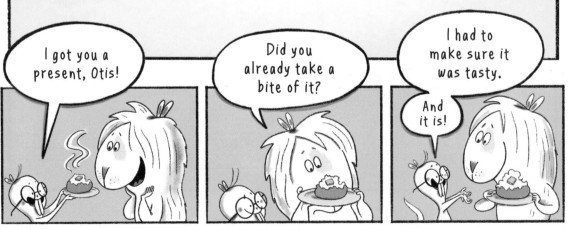